Haunting
CONCLUSIONS

Also by Phyllis Eickelberg

Bearly Hidden, 2011
Desperate Measures, 2012

Haunting
CONCLUSIONS

A BRAIN TEASER MYSTERY

Phyllis Eickelberg

abbott press®

A DIVISION OF WRITER'S DIGEST

Haunting Conclusions
A Brain Teaser Mystery

Abbott Press books may be ordered through booksellers or by contacting:

Abbott Press
1663 Liberty Drive
Bloomington, IN 47403
www.abbottpress.com
Phone: 1-866-697-5310

ISBN: 978-1-4582-0841-5 (sc)
ISBN: 978-1-4582-0840-8 (e)

Library of Congress Control Number: 2013903658

Printed in the United States of America

Abbott Press rev. date: 3/4/2013

PUZZLE MENU

ACKNOWLEDGEMENTS:

The author wishes to express a special debt of gratitude once more—to her husband Jim, who continues being patient and helpful—each time dinner's late.

Thanks, too, to proofreaders and consultants Julie Searcy, Katie Cooper, Stacy Mellem, Ben Wolcott, Peter Saunders, Doris Cameron-Minard, Sam Hall, Frank Yates, Alison Hopkins, Tandy Tillinghast, Anne Chaimov, Rosemary Cunningham, Janice Fisher, Susan Pachuta, Carolyn Hegstad, Robin Suzanne, Peter and Mariana Burke, Dinaz Rogers, Jason Schindler, Dennis Stillwagon, Clinton Morrison, Nancy Jamison, John and Kathe Burk, and to Steve and Michelle Holmquist for solving various computer and story problems for me

Thanks also to Dr. Steven Eickelberg for some medical direction, and to Jim Searcy for information concerning how to discover bad accounting practices.

Rendezvous, Revenge, and Revealed secrets

A broken leg, a thief in disguise, a double agent, and someone about to die; Heather's life has never been so exciting.

What she *didn't* expect was to get involved in the lives of her neighbors. What she *did* expect was to contribute one helpful moment, then get back to solving the mysteries haunting her family.

But that one helpful moment turned her life upside down.

Will she be able to find answers without more complications? Or more murders? Time is running out.

Haunting Conclusions is a story of intrigue, subterfuge and some long-awaited answers.

HERE WE GO

A = N and N = A

A B C D E F G H I J K L M
N O P Q R S T U V W X Y Z

PUVYYVAT ZBGVIRF CERINVY

<u>C</u> _ _ _ _ _   _ _ _ _ _ _   _ _ _ _ _ _

CHAPTER 1

The conspirators sat at a table, their heads close, voices little more than whispers.

"Of course I'll do away with her if I get the chance." With a thumb and middle finger measuring a distance of half an inch, the speaker continued, "I'm this close to finding her." Pushing away from the table, the would-be killer stood, stretching tired muscles.

"Is revenge worth going to prison?" his friend asked.

"Who said anything about getting caught?"

"If you're going to avoid that you'll have to design a plan that's foolproof, and I may not be able to help you this time."

A smirk lit the killer's face. "Not to worry. Murder and design are my specialties. Now let's figure out a way to get listening devices into the Samuelson house."

###

"I'm glad you could both join me this morning." Heather Samuelson pushed a strand of auburn hair behind one ear as she sat opposite her sisters at the dining room table. "I thought I'd have unlimited time this morning, but I don't. I have to leave in an hour." She glanced at her watch.

Across the table, Sally, the youngest of the three sisters and an officer in the Lewisburg Police Department, quietly filed her nails. Rachel, the middle sister and mother of ten-year-old twins was biting hers.

"I want to discuss Mom's letter." Heather referred to the letter their mother's attorney turned over to her soon after Mattie's death in February.

"Have you solved the letter's puzzles?" Rachel, prematurely gray and two years younger than thirty-year-old-Heather, leaned forward. She frowned when her sister shook her head. "But you're close, aren't you?"

"I think so." Heather put a folder on the table and pulled a list from it. "That's why I wanted this meeting—to see what you think of my theories."

"Mom obviously wanted us to know something she didn't feel comfortable writing out in plain English." Sally put her nail file away and reached for her coffee. "I hope you've figured out what her letter is trying to tell us."

Heather studied her sisters' expectant faces. "I think I have some of the answers; so let's get cracking." She shifted in her chair, pencil poised.

In February the attorney for Mattie Samuelson's estate had given a sealed envelope and a wrapped package to Heather. Mattie's instructions, according to the attorney, were that Heather share the contents of both only with her sisters, but not until after their mother's memorial service. He added that Mattie had updated the documents every September for eight years. Nearly a year had now passed since she last made changes.

"Before we start, read Mom's letter again," Sally said.

Rachel shivered. "It always gives me the creeps."

Heather pulled the letter from her file, cleared her throat, and began reading:

> "My Darling Girls,
>
> "If you are reading this it means you've saved the desk, and I'm not around to explain any of its contents, or to tell any more grandbabies those wonderful puzzle stories that young Tim and Tom loved to hear me invent. I'm sorry. I wish I was still with you. Instead I will leave you with my newest and last fairytale. Your puzzle satisfaction will be based on your own inventiveness, but then that is Heather's hobby, isn't it! And if Sally will quietly do nothing, then Rachel can take up the telling of this story to any new grandbabies. I send you love.
>
> "Once upon a time in the land of long ago,
> Lived a grownup Cinderella whose story you should know.
>
> "After Cindy's shoe was restored, she and Prince Charming married and were living happily ever after with the sweetest babies any parent could hope for.

Prince Charming was ruling his divisional kingdom of the faithful and the truthful, lending others his skills as they had need of them.

"Unfortunately, Prince Charming discovered he was sharing his skills with the Big Bad Wolf.

"It turned out that BB Wolf wasn't just huffing and puffing on the doorstep of the three little pigs; he was hurting everyone in the forest except himself. The Prince talked the matter over with the Game Warden who promised to put Big Bad into a cage so others would be safe. Of course the Prince would have to tell the whole world about Big Bad's treacherous ways.

"To everyone's chagrin Big Bad had evil friends. He also had wonderful gifts for those friends, if, while he was trying to get his cage door open, they would do away with the Prince as punishment for tattling. He also wanted bad things to happen to anyone who had a hand in putting him in that cage even though it was his own evil deeds that caused him to be there.

"To save Prince Charming, the Game Warden sent him to a safe tower where he couldn't be found. If Big Bad got the cage door open, the Prince would again have to help cage him. Big Bad's evil friends were frustrated when they couldn't find Prince Charming, so they decided to do away with Cinderella. They knew **that** would bring the Prince out of hiding and to her bedside.

"And for a brief moment, it worked.

"Soon after that Big Bad heard that Prince Charming did a 'Humpty Dumpty.' Knowing he was dead satisfied Big Bad's urge to kill him so Cindy and the babies were left alone and Big Bad's evil friends chased after the others on the hit list.

"Most of Prince Charming's family learned to live happily ever after without him because they were becoming adults and learning to find their own way through the forest.

"Now then, whether the Kings Men are successful in putting the egg shells back together, is yet to be seen. Whether the grown babies get to applaud and view the completed eggshell puzzle is also undetermined.

"May you all live Happily Ever After!

"PS: On a lighter note, I recommend some of the vacation locations I have visited over the last few years. They are not the usual places to visit, but each has its own charm. These were Montgomery, Juneau, Phoenix, Little Rock, Sacramento, Denver, and Hartford."

When Heather finished reading she noted the sad faces across from her. Their mother's untimely death still troubled them. "Okay. As we know, Mom always said that in case of a fire we were to save her writing desk first."

Sally nodded. "And we know now it held only a few legal papers, a scrapbook and a bundle of birthday cards tied together with a red ribbon."

Rachel interrupted. "And the postmarks on the cards indicate Mom received a card each year over the last eight years. We know Dad didn't send them, even though it looks like his handwriting."

The problem with crediting the cards to their father was that he had died nine years earlier, while taking part in a search and rescue mission on Mt. Hood. A winter storm's white-out made it difficult for the searchers to see. As a result Charlie lost his footing and slipped into a glacial crevasse so deep and narrow his body couldn't be recovered.

Heather checked an item from her list. "Mom's attorney told us to wait until after her memorial service to read her letter. I think that's because by then, we would have received that flower arrangement that arrived with a personal message and an unsigned card."

Rachel said, "That's crazy. Mom would have to know before she died that there'd *be* unidentified flowers. You're not making sense."

"I think Mom knew the sender so well it was a given." Heather checked another item off her list.

Rachel sighed. "Go ahead. I can accept that."

"Next point! Mom's letter mentions puzzle stories she told the twins and we know that didn't happen. I think she put that in her letter as an excuse for what follows, in case the wrong people got hold of the letter. I'm betting once we decode it, we'll learn a secret so important that Mom needed to make sure no one else would figure it out."

"She knew you could unravel it," Rachel said. "But why did she add that part about Sally?"

"I'm to *quietly do nothing,*" Sally responded. "Heather thinks that means I am not to use department resources to search for information."

"Why would Mom limit you in that way?" Rachel asked.

"We don't know yet," Sally explained. "But for the moment we're honoring her request."

A sad smile crossed Heather's face. "As we come up with new theories, the temptation to use Sally's resources gets harder to resist."

"Okay. So Mom didn't invent fairy tales for the twins, but she obviously invented one for her daughters." Rachel laughed.

Heather shook her head "I don't agree. I don't think Mom's letter *is* a fairy tale. I think it's a true story. About her and Dad."

###

ADVICE FOR THE SAMUELSONS

P + 3 =	D + 4 =	G - 6 =	L + 2 =
P + 4 =	K + 4 =	P + 4 =	G + 2 =
D - 3 =	P - 3 =		D + 3 =
W + 2 =	A + 4 =		K - 3 =
			P + 4 =

<u>S</u> _ _ _   _ _ _ _   _ _   _ _ _ _ _

CHAPTER 2

"We've discussed the possibility that it's a real life story before," Sally said.

"For the moment, let's assume that's what it is, and move on. Here's what I think happened. I think Dad had a client who broke the law and Dad blew the whistle."

"That would account for Mom's reference to the game warden," Sally said. "It would mean Dad consulted the authorities."

"Exactly." Heather nodded. "I think there was a trial and Dad was a witness—*telling the world about his client's crime.* I think Mr. Big Bad Wolf was found guilty."

Sally had a thoughtful look on her face again. "If you're right, that reference to him trying to get out of his cage probably refers to the appeals process. Dad's former client must have appealed his conviction."

Heather nodded. "It may be that Dad's client is *still* appealing his conviction. The appeals process can go on for years while hearing dates are scheduled and rescheduled, with claims of being denied a fair trial evaluated."

Sally nodded slowly.

"If our hunch is correct and Big Bad is still appealing his conviction, then the next point in Mom's story may also still be happening."

"And the next point is?" Rachel asked, elbows on the table, her head resting in cupped hands.

Heather explained, "What's next is that Dad's former client may have hired someone to kill those who helped put him in jail."

Sally and Rachel focused startled looks on their sister.

Heather said, "The letter says, Big Bad wanted bad things to happen to anyone who had a hand in putting him in that cage."

"Recap," whispered Sally leaning back in her chair. "Let's assume you're right. Let's assume that without Dad's testimony Big Bad wouldn't have gone to jail."

"Keep going." Heather nodded encouragement.

"If Big Bad wins an appeal and is released or gets a new trial scheduled, then . . . ," Sally paused.

Heather nodded, "Then, if it was Dad's testimony that clinched the first conviction . . . ."

". . . then the prosecution might put Dad some place where Big Bad and his buddies couldn't find him." Sally looked up to see her sister nodding enthusiastically. "The Witness Protection Program?"

"Wait a minute." Rachel jumped to her feet and began pacing. "You're going too fast for me to take all this in."

Heather said, "I think there came a time when the bad guys couldn't find Dad, and they decided to draw him out of hiding by attacking Cinderella."

"Oh no!" Rachel's hands flew to her face, her eyes wide. "You're thinking about Mom's fall. When she tumbled down those stairs at the train station we accused her of being clumsy, but she always said someone tried to kill her." Tears filled Rachel's eyes.

Mattie's fall had been serious enough to cripple her so that she couldn't manage alone. She'd left the hospital and moved to an assisted living facility.

Heather said, "I suspect Dad came out of hiding to be at Mom's bedside while she was in the hospital, and that made him vulnerable."

"And they killed him? Do you think his fall on the mountain wasn't an accident?" Rachel pressed a tissue against her eyes.

"Calm down, Sis. Let's consider an alternative. What if the members of that search and rescue team were the good guys? What if the reference to Prince Charming doing a 'Humpty Dumpty' refers . . ."

". . . to Dad's fall," Sally added. "We already know that, but if the fall was faked . . ." She left the sentence unfinished, staring at Heather with wide eyes.

Heather nodded, whispering, "Then Dad might still be alive."

The room suddenly became quiet, a chill in the air.

"And," Heather continued softly, "if he's alive, he'd be able to send cards and flowers to Mom in a style she'd recognize."

"We'd recognize it, too," Sally added. "But Mom never showed us those cards."

"Dad can't be in the Witness Protection Program," Rachel said. "That's for entire families."

"Think about it, Rachel. They couldn't put all of us in Witness Protection. It would mean your husband had to find a new job and change his name. Your boys would have new names, and Sally and I . . ." Heather left the thought incomplete. It was too many people to relocate. The way to keep everyone safe was to stage the death of the prime target.

"Would Mom have agreed to stay behind? Wouldn't she go with Dad?" Sally asked.

"To begin with, she was in the hospital for weeks, and while she was there, Dad had his fall. I think she'd already made the decision to act the part of a grieving widow to take the heat off of Dad." Heather checked one more point off her list.

"But they worshipped each other. Mom and Dad had been sweethearts forever. How could she stand to be separated from him?" Rachel asked.

"I guess you have to love someone enough that you can let them go." Heather looked up. "Let's talk about that later and move on to Mom's scrapbook." She picked up the book they'd found in their mother's desk, and opened it at a page containing a newspaper story of a murder trial. The guilty man had left the courtroom, threatening everyone involved in his trial. Heather passed the scrapbook across the table to her sisters so they could scan the article.

When the scrapbook had been discovered, the sisters tried to understand why their mother kept an accounting of a trial they'd never heard of, along with a collection of obituaries for people they didn't know. None of the sisters had been in Oregon when the Joel Bishop trial took place.

Rachel stopped turning pages and pointed to a death notice concerning a fisherman who drowned. "I remember this story," she said. "What's it doing in Mom's scrapbook? It happened five months after she died."

"I put it there because it's related to the Bishop trial," Heather explained. "That fisherman was the trial judge. I added his obituary to Mom's collection because I think all those obituaries may be people who took part in that trial."

"Then you think the Big Bad Wolf and," Rachel glanced at the newspaper clipping, "and Joel Bishop are the same person?"

Heather nodded. "I did some investigating a month ago. Newspaper records at the library said Mr. Bishop was on trial first for embezzlement, something Dad would have been involved in. During that trial Bishop's wife and her children by a previous marriage died when their car went over a cliff. Their brake line had been cut. The prosecution charged Bishop with cutting it to keep his wife from telling where the embezzled funds were hidden. Bishop was found guilty of embezzlement and in a later trial, guilty of the murders. He's currently serving a life sentence without the possibility of parole."

"Can he still appeal?" Rachel asked.

"Oh yes," Sally responded.

"If his threat as he left the court wasn't an idle one," Heather continued, "then there may have been a hit list, and a hired killer."

Sally shivered. "We need to see who was on those juries, and compare their names with people whose obituaries Mom collected."

Heather smiled at her sisters and marked off another point on her list. "I tried that. A couple of months ago I applied for information concerning jury members in Bishop's trials."

"And?" Sally asked.

"And had a visit from a federal agent who told me I would not be permitted to have that information because of the threat Mr. Bishop made."

"The FBI came to see you?" Sally looked surprised.

"I think the man who showed up was a U.S. Marshal. It occurs to me someone slipped up when they sent him, unless they wanted us to connect him with the Witness Protection Program. It's the U.S. Marshals who monitor it."

"Even if I tried to use department resources to ask questions about that program, no one would answer me. It's considered top secret." Sally paused, "Mom would have known that, so why tell me to quietly do nothing, unless she thought someone in local law enforcement works for Bishop. Do you think that's why she didn't want me asking questions at the station?"

Heather nodded. "Until we know better, I think we have to consider that possibility. Now then, remember the package Mom's attorney gave me? It's supposed to be a jigsaw puzzle of the United States."

Rachel looked up. "Why would Mom want that to be a secret?"

"Why indeed? The puzzle pieces are all blank." Heather laughed. "Identifying marks have been torn off all of them, and some pieces are actually missing. If the puzzle pieces weren't shaped like individual states, I wouldn't be able to fit them together to discover which ones were missing."

"Blank puzzle pieces? That doesn't make sense," Rachel said. "Do you think Mom was losing it?"

"I think Mom did that so we'd pay close attention to the final paragraph in her letter—the one talking about vacations. Look at the suggestions she's made: Montgomery, Juneau, Phoenix, Little Rock, Sacramento, Denver, and Hartford. Those locations have three things in common."

"They're all state capitals," Rachel exclaimed. She'd helped her twins memorize state capitals a year ago.

"True. They also represent, in alphabetical order, the first seven of our fifty states. Coincidentally, those are the seven states whose pieces are missing from the puzzle." Heather looked at her sisters' frustrated expressions. "Do you know what the next alphabetical state is?

"Delaware?"

"Right."

"Why is that important?" Rachel asked.

"After Mom died, I kept her wall calendar. It had beautiful pictures of Connecticut when the leaves turn, and of the Atlantic coastline. Think of Connecticut as state number seven on this list. I've been using Mom's calendar since her death in February. Imagine my surprise when the page for September was turned up, and I found Mom has a reservation of some kind for two weeks from today."

"In Delaware?" Sally rubbed her forehead, pushing hair aside.

"I don't know where. There's a reservation number written on the fifteenth of September, and that's all. I didn't find it in February when I cancelled her other appointments."

"How will you find out what the reservation is for?" Rachel asked.

"Tomorrow I start calling Dover, Delaware, motels. If I can track down the one expecting Mom, then in two weeks I'm going to Delaware."

Sally smiled, anticipating her sister's plan.

"I don't understand," Rachel said. "Why would you go to Delaware? For what purpose?"

"Assuming I'm right about all of this and that Mom and Dad worked together creating her letter and its puzzles, then in two weeks I expect to be spending some quality time with Dad."

DANGER CREEPS CLOSER

	1	2	3	4	5	6	7	8
A	M	F	T	E	E	W	L	D
B	D	U	H	B	A	T	B	C
C	K	C	S	S	J	X	Q	P
D	J	E	Z	Y	G	I	R	G
E	M	T	N	S	O	E	N	L
F	R	B	A	G	H	Y	I	N
G	O	C	T	Y	O	O	A	H
H	P	A	I	D	T	L	B	E

B5   C1, D6, A7, H6, A4, F1   F7, C3   G2, H6, G1, C4, H8

<u>A</u> _ _ _ _ _   _ _   _ _ _ _ _

CHAPTER 3

The meeting with her sisters ended and Heather rushed to keep an appointment with one of her housing association's Board of Directors.

"These street lights absolutely have to be checked tonight or we'll have more break-ins." Brad Keyes, a neighbor of Heather's, gestured at one of the tall lamp posts that needed to be monitored. It stood near the intersection of the association's main road and one of the fire lanes leading to homeowner carports. When he asked for help, Heather had reluctantly volunteered.

She sighed. "Break-ins? Sally and I moved here two months ago because we thought this was a safe neighborhood."

"It *is* safe when our security system works, but when it doesn't, thieves show up."

"Why are *we* checking street lights? Why isn't someone from the city doing that?"

"Our streets and our street lights weren't built to city specifications, so we can't deed them to Lewisburg. That means the upkeep and care belongs to people who live here." He handed Heather a small slip of paper with crosses on it. It looked like a child's sketch of a graveyard.

"This is a map of our security system. Wait until dark; then check the lights. They're all on solar timers and have new bulbs in them. If a light isn't lit, circle it on the map. I'll need to get an electrician to check it out."

It seemed easy as Brad explained the task that morning, but by the time it was dark enough to check the lights, September's blue sky had filled with dark clouds and rain.

Heather shivered as she followed Brad's map, and when a bolt of lightning cut through the night sky, she paused. *One thousand one, one thousand two.* There were three more lights to be checked before she could get out of the rain.

She approached the intersection near Brad's street, aware that the street light was out. Earlier Brad had said, *"Sometimes you have to reach up and tap the fixture."*

Heather closed her umbrella, and reached up, thumping the dark post. Big drops fell from the wet umbrella, and she gasped, brushing water from her head. The street light remained dark, but a flash of light from the house closest to her caught her attention.

Whoever lived next door to Brad, at the end of his street, was moving around indoors with a flashlight.

Heather watched the light's path through the house as it reflected off the windows. Suddenly she recalled Brad's comment about break-ins. Cautiously Heather moved to one of the home's undraped windows. She raised her flashlight, pressed it against the glass, and briefly flicked it on, then off.

"Oh no," she gasped, her voice a whisper. The room into which her light flashed had been ravaged. Glass doors on a hutch were shattered, drawers were missing, and debris scattered.

Heather crouched at the side of the house and pulled out her cell phone. She pushed the speed dial for nine-one-one, and responded to the operator, "Yes, it's an emergency. There's a burglary in progress."

###

A LOOK AHEAD

For the Experienced Detective Only

Below is a crazy quilt of words. Each can be found in an irregular configuration. Move from letter to letter vertically or horizontally; not diagonally. Each letter is used only once. There's one more word in the chart than is listed. Can you find it? It may be important.

ACCIDENT, BISHOP, CHARLIE, CINDERELLA,
ESCAPES, HITMAN, MURDERER, PRINCE,
SECRETS, THIEVES, TRIAL, WARDEN

A	C	C	I	C	H	A	R	C	I	N
W	A	E	D	B	E	I	L	R	E	D
D	R	N	S	I	A	L	L	E	M	U
E	N	T	H	O	P	R	R	E	D	R
H	I	T	M	P	N	I	E	R	V	E
T	R	N	A	E	C	T	H	I	E	S
A	I	L	E	E	A	P	S	E	C	R
L	M	O	S	S	C	E	S	S	T	E

###

"You really got things stirred up last night," Brad congratulated Heather the next morning. They were standing beside the burgled house. "I couldn't believe all the flashing, swirling lights outside my door. Too bad the guy got away." In his bright yellow, too-long raincoat, Brad, short to start with, looked like one of the seven dwarfs on construction duty.

The wind shifted and Heather pulled the hood of her coat closer to her face. "Sally and I haven't been here long enough to meet everyone, so I didn't know who lived here."

"The house is owned by Doc Adams," Brad said. "I could at least tell the cops that much, but in the five years I've lived here, I've never met him or the woman renting his house. I'm not even sure what her name is."

"That's unusual, isn't it? After all, she's your next door neighbor."

Brad nodded. "It's very unusual. Our neighborhood gossips don't know anything about her, and their get-acquainted parties haven't lured her out of her house." He laughed. "I suspect they have a game of twenty questions planned for her."

"Hasn't anyone talked to Doc Adams about his tenant?"

"No one at Taborhill Garden Estates has. Doc's in a nursing home. As long as the house is kept up, we have no quarrel with who comes and goes." Brad raised his hand and waved at his daughter as she pedaled away on her bike. "You've met Stormy, haven't you?"

Heather nodded. "She stopped by and introduced herself. I understand she's looking for part time work."

"College expenses are the pits. We can use every penny we can lay our hands on." Brad thrust his hands into cold pockets.

Heather shifted to accommodate another change in the wind's direction. At that moment a truck with *Aba Brothers Electrical* pulled up. "Here's your electrician," she said, reaching into her pocket for the map of lamp posts. "Only the last three still need to be checked." She extended the map toward Brad.

He shook his head. "Please finish checking. I can assume responsibility again tomorrow, but not tonight." He turned to greet the electrician. "I have to make sure Leonardo gets this light repaired. He's been careless about it. That's why there was a burglary here last night."

Heather nodded. "It sounds like this place isn't as crime-free as Sally and I thought."

Heather settled at her computer, surfing through font options for one that fit her client's website. Coffman Jewelers hired her to get their website up and running, but they kept insisting on changes.

The phone rang and Heather flicked a switch so she could continue working as she talked. "Samuelson Design Services, Heather speaking."

"You sound so professional," laughed Sally. "I'm sorry to interrupt, but I thought you might like to volunteer for another job."

"There's that word again." Heather frowned, backspacing to correct a spelling error. "Whatever you're about to suggest, the answer is

NOPE. I don't volunteer any more. Don't you have crimes to solve? Why are you interrupting me?"

"It's your own fault. If you hadn't discovered the B&E last night, there wouldn't be anything I'd like your assistance with."

"Okay! Explain yourself!"

"I stopped at The Boardwalk Nursing Home and tried unsuccessfully to talk to Doc Adams. Until we get in touch with the woman renting his house, we won't know if anything was taken. Could you glance that way a few times today, in case she shows up? Maybe look that way when you need a break. If anything seems to be going on, give me a call."

"Okay! I can do that." Heather turned her attention back to testing font styles. "Since The Boardwalk's in Harrison County and not in your jurisdiction, I'm assuming you asked county cops to call on Doc Adams for you. Did they turn you down?"

Sally laughed. "On the contrary. They said they'd be glad to chat with him after they solve a murder and find the gang that robbed their bank last week. They mentioned something about doing it after their union negotiates a big raise, but by then I'd stopped listening."

Heather laughed. "What a helpful group." A burring sound caused her to jump to her feet. "Gotta go, Sis. Someone's at the front door. Let me get a few things finished for Coffman Jewelers; then I'll check out the neighborhood."

Heather hung up and rushed down the stairs.

The handsome man at her front door had a helmet in his hand. Behind him, a motorcycle was in the carport. "Hi, Beautiful. I've got a couple hours of free time. Need a strong arm to assist with anything?"

"Jazz." Heather smiled and stepped aside. "Come in."

Madison County's undercover deputy, James Finchum, known to everyone as Jazz, had met Heather soon after her mother died. "What are you up to?" he asked, following her indoors.

"I'm still working on the Coffman Jewelers account, but I'm due for a break." She sighed. "Will you have coffee or tea?"

"Coffee, if it's handy. You're never involved in just one thing. What else is going on?" Jazz followed Heather to the kitchen where a freshly perked pot of coffee waited. Heather filled two mugs, pushing one across the table to him.

"We had a burglary last night, a couple of doors away."

"Do our city cops have a lead on who's responsible?"

Heather shook her head. "Until they find the woman who lives in the burgled house, they won't know if anything was taken. Sally asked me to keep an eye on the place in case the renter shows up. It's owned by a man who's a patient at The Boardwalk. What I'd really like to do is talk to him. He apparently wouldn't answer when Sally questioned him earlier."

"Jump on the back of my bike. I can have you there in five minutes. It's not raining at the moment."

"Really? Great! Finish your coffee while I turn off my computer."

"Don't forget your helmet," Jazz reminded her as she vanished up the stairs.

He paced the floor as he waited. He'd had an early morning conversation with Sergeant Richard (Ox) Miller, his partner for the last few months. If they were right and the number of those who took part in Joel Bishop's trials was dwindling, then the threat Bishop made as he left the courtroom hadn't been an idle one.

What troubled Jazz was the possibility that the man who started the investigations, Charlie Samuelson, wasn't dead. If Bishop's assassin got wind of that, he might go after Charlie's daughters in an attempt to lure Charlie out of hiding.

Jazz was staying close. The sisters might need protection.

###

WHO NEEDS MONEY?

A, A, B, B, D, E, M, R, Y

Using each of the above letters only once, add one to <u>each</u> word below, forming a new word. The addition may be at the beginning, end, or within the word. Place the added letter on the line below the boxes. The added letters, reading from left to right, will form a 4-letter and a 5-letter word that answers the title question.

ice	rod	ear	rave	hat
mice				

<u>   M   </u>_____

one	thee	red	bear
bone			

<u>   B   </u>_____

CHAPTER 4

Heather left Jazz standing beside his motorcycle when she entered The Boardwalk. "I'd like to see Doctor Adams," she explained to the admitting nurse.

"That's Doc Adams. It's a nickname; not a title. He's awake now and would probably appreciate a visitor." She pointed to her left. "Follow this hall until you get to the first right turn. Room 465 will be on the left."

Heather walked quickly, pausing at the entrance to Room 465. "May I come in?" She could see two occupied beds in the dimly lighted room.

"Come! Come!" called the occupant of the bed closest to the door.

Heather entered. "Are you Doc Adams?"

"We've never met before, have we?" The old man laughed. Steely blue eyes sparkled from a face with an impish grin.

"No, we haven't," agreed Heather moving closer to the bed.

"Well, you've found me. Who are you and what can I do for you?" A skinny arm with a bandaged wrist was thrust in Heather's direction.

"I won't keep you long, Mr. Adams," Heather said, shaking hands. "My name's Heather Samuelson."

"Call me Doc. Everyone does." The old man laughed. "What's a cute chick like you want with an old duffer like me?" His voice dropped to a whisper, and he pulled bedding closer to his thin face. "You got any pills on you?"

"No pills." Heather shook her head. "I'm here about the house you own at Taborhill Garden Estates. It was burglarized last night. Your property wasn't harmed, but your renter's things were damaged."

"Sorry to hear that. Why don't you sit down and fill me in on all the details? Are you sure you don't have an aspirin or something?"

Heather shook her head and continued, "The problem the police are having is that there's no record of who your renter is or how to contact her."

"And they sent a pretty little thing like you to get that information? Why didn't the cops come in person?"

"Jake Lundeen!" A nurse stood in the doorway, her fists resting on ample hips. "Are you pretending to be Doc Adams again? This lady doesn't have any meds for you to steal, so let her see the person she came here to visit."

Heather looked at the man the nurse had called Jake Lundeen. "You're not Doc Adams?"

"Who you gonna believe? Her or me?" He laughed with a high-pitched cackle. "Hey, Doc," he shouted. "Get a load'a this one."

Heather walked to the second bed and looked at the man whose emaciated frame displayed enough bones to lose count. "Doc Adams?" she asked softly.

"Who wants to know?" His eyes remained closed.

"My name is Heather Samuelson. I live near your property in Taborhill. I need to know the name of your renter and how to get in touch with her."

"Can't," he whispered. "You gotta wait for Inez to get in touch."

"She must send rent checks. Isn't there some contact information on those?"

"She only sends cashier's checks, or big bundles of cash." For the first time Doc became animated. His eyelids snapped open.

"What's her last name? Where does she work?"

Doc giggled. "That's one lady with really good hands. Sends me cash." His animation began to fade. He yawned, "Gonna catch a little more shut-eye." His eyelids shut again.

"What's Inez's last name?" Heather asked again. "Where does she work?"

Doc Adams responded with dainty snoring sounds much like soup bubbling on the stove.

The nurse finished with Jake Lundeen and moved to check on Doc Adams. "You'll have better luck talking to his son," she said softly.

"He handles Doc's business affairs now." She reached in her pocket, removed a pad, and jotted a name. "You'll find him at the church on Emerson Street." She handed Heather the paper. On it was written, *Father Raymond Adams.*

###

WHAT TIME IS IT?

	1	2	3	4	5	6	7	8
A	V	M	T	S	D	V	O	I
B	R	C	P	B	M	G	K	E
C	H	S	T	E	N	N	F	A
D	R	E	R	U	O	L	J	R

A3, A8, B5, D2, A3, D5 A4, C3, A7, B3
A3, C1, D2 A2, D4, B1, A5, D2, D8

– – –   – –   – – – –   – – –   – – – – – –

###

St. Mary's Church was a sprawling building that included a day care center for adults needing assistance on a day-to-day basis. The center took over nursing duties so caregivers could enjoy a respite day. Snacks were being served as Heather and Jazz entered. When they asked to see Father Adams, they were sent to a room off the main sanctuary where a man with closely-cropped gray hair sat reading.

"May I help you?" he asked when Heather and Jazz approached him. He had intense brown eyes and a smile that seemed frozen in place. He gestured toward a bench opposite his desk.

"I need to contact the woman who rents your father's house in Taborhill Garden Estates," Heather said. "It was broken into last night. Until the police talk to the lady renting the property, they won't know if anything is missing. I just visited your father and he . . ."

"And he stopped in the middle of a sentence and fell asleep."

Heather nodded.

"If you saw Dad, you must have met Jake Lundeen." Father Adams laughed when he saw Heather's grinning response. "Did he get any pills from you?"

"None."

"I usually take small peppermints when I visit Dad. Jake accepts them as pills and the nursing staff has approved them. Want a peppermint?" He indicated a capped container on his desk. When his offer was declined he leaned back in his chair and studied the couple across from him. "So you want to know how to find Inez Perkins?"

"Perkins," Heather sighed. "Your dad only told me her first name."

"I've been sorting through his personal papers, otherwise I wouldn't know it." Father Adams' smile broadened. "Dad seems to be right about not being able to contact her. She travels and only gets in touch if she has questions or needs something."

"How often is that?" Heather asked.

"Every decade or so, as near as I can tell."

Heather gave the priest a startled look. "She must have some way to check for messages if only to make sure there's a building for her to return to."

Father Adams shrugged his shoulders. "I can't answer that. Apparently thirty or forty years ago, Inez and Dad crossed paths. She volunteered to buy a house and put his name on the deed if he'd let her live in it, no questions asked."

Jazz interrupted, "The house was paid for by Perkins, but the deed was put in your dad's name?"

Father Adams nodded.

"Amazing!" Heather said.

Father Adams nodded again. "She sends money for taxes, insurance, utilities, and any upkeep the place needs. It's always in cash or a cashier's check. She doesn't pay rent and there's no mortgage."

"Your dad and Inez must be close friends," Jazz said. "They obviously trust each other."

"Except for the house, I haven't discovered any other connection."

"I don't understand buying a house and deeding it to someone else," Heather said.

"Apparently Inez does charitable things. After Dad dies, she gets to live in the house until her death. Then it passes to the church, free and clear. The house hasn't cost Dad a cent and Inez has lived in it since it was built thirty-some years ago."

"Let me get this straight," Jazz said. "Ms. Perkins has a place to live, with no insurance or property tax records in her name. Right?"

Father Adams nodded.

"Who gets the tax advantage?" Jazz asked.

"Dad does."

"They must have known each other long before they set up a business relationship like the one you described," Heather said.

"When I can get Dad to talk about it, he claims to have been walking home from the store one day when Inez approached him and suggested they sit down and chat."

"And after a cup of coffee she trusted him enough to buy a house and put the deed in his name?" Heather looked at Jazz and saw her disbelief mirrored there.

"With Dad, it's sometimes hard to tell if it's a story he's making up, or something he's recalling from his past." Father Adams continued, "However it came together, the tax deduction credits helped Dad get on his feet financially. He had a hard time until Inez showed up. He's never been clear about when or where he met her, but I know she's been the house's only occupant." Puzzled faces stared at him. "I don't know anything else about the transaction. I was away at seminary at the time and when I finished there, I went to England."

"You're managing your dad's estate now, but haven't found any way to contact his tenant?" Jazz asked.

"None. I doubt she knows Dad's in such poor health. During the twelve years that I've been involved, she hasn't been in touch once."

"How does she know the property tax amount?" Heather asked.

"I have no idea. That woman and her arrangements are total mysteries to me."

###

"I'm sorry your trip to The Boardwalk didn't produce answers," Sally said. Heather was carrying plates of seafood salad to the dinner table.

"Thankfully, Father Adams knew the renter's name, but he didn't know a whole lot more." Heather passed salad dressing to her sister and sat down.

"The arrangement between Doc Adams and Inez Perkins sounds like something fishy is going on. And that's not just a cop talking." Sally took a bite of salad and chewed thoughtfully for a minute.

"Were you able to find out anything about her?"

Sally shook her head. "She doesn't show up anywhere, not even on a driver's license. At the very least she sounds like an undisclosed principal. If she bought property and put it in someone else's name, how would she know they wouldn't sell it and keep the proceeds?"

"Jazz and I asked that question."

"But didn't get an answer? It's a good thing you like puzzles. Are you having any luck tracing Mom's reservation? You only have thirteen days left."

"I've started calling motels close to Dover's small airports, although I suspect there isn't much traffic in or out of them. Most people flying to that location probably use the Baltimore airport."

"Do you have lamp post duty again tonight?" Sally pushed her empty plate away.

"I wish I didn't, but Brad gets his job checking on lights back in the morning, after I check out three more." Heather picked up her flashlight and the security system map, then reached for her coat. "Where's that pencil?" She patted her coat pockets.

"There's one poking out of your right pocket." Sally glanced at her watch. "Only three lamp posts, huh? Why don't I do that for you? After all, you helped me out today."

"Would you?" Heather located the pencil and handed it to Sally. "That would free me to get into my pajamas and work comfortably."

Sally slipped her raincoat on. She studied the crude map briefly, then stuffed the flashlight and the pencil in a pocket. With an umbrella ready to unfurl, she headed for the door.

"Thanks," Heather said, giving her sister a hug.

Sally opened the door and stepped out into the rain. "I just wish it wasn't so dark and so wet."

###

Because the TGE association's fire lanes had never been named, it was nearly impossible to go directly to an unfamiliar location without getting lost, especially at night. The fire lanes all led to carports and intersected only with the main road. Unfortunately the fire lanes all looked alike—as did the townhouses.

Sally located two of the lamp posts that needed to be checked, but in the darkness and heavy rain, the third one wasn't obvious. She tried to get her bearings, but the weather and the darkness were disorienting. When she came to an empty carport, she stepped into it, collapsing her umbrella. With the aid of Heather's dim flashlight she studied the map. It looked like the remaining lamp post should be close to her present location, but except for a few porch lights, the area around her was dark. Either the street light wasn't working, or she wasn't where she'd first thought. Before she could be sure of her location, the flashlight blinked off.

"Of course this couldn't be easy," she mumbled, shaking the light to see if it would turn on again. When it didn't, she stuffed it in a wet coat pocket, an action that caused her to drop the map.

Sally knelt quickly, trying to find the paper before the wind carried it away. When her cell phone rang, she got to her feet and pulled the phone from her jean's pocket.

"Hello," she said, kneeling again to search for the map. "Speak up."

One hand held the phone and the other searched the dark asphalt for the map. With her attention divided, she was unaware of a slow moving vehicle traveling only with its parking lights on. The vehicle turned from the fire lane into the dark carport where Sally searched for the map.

Too late, the driver saw a figure bent over the ground. Brakes were slammed on, but the impact sent Sally sprawling.

Headlights came on, and the driver rushed to Sally's side. "Dear God, I didn't see you. Are you all right?"

Sally moaned. One leg was twisted at an odd angle.

"Can you put your arm around my neck and turn over? I need to take you to the hospital."

"Get . . . Heather," Sally moaned.

"Where is Heather?"

"6-6-7-3."

"I know where that is. Don't move. I'll get her." The woman rushed off.

Impatient knocking began just as Heather stepped into her pajamas. Thinking Sally was having trouble with her key, Heather hurried down the stairs without grabbing her robe.

On her doorstep stood a woman of average height, beautifully dressed except for occasional splatters of mud.

"Yes?" Heather inquired.

"Are you Heather?" The woman was breathing hard, wringing her hands, and nervously glancing behind her.

"Yes, I'm Heather. Could you come in so I can close the door and get my robe?"

"I can't come in. I need you to come out. I just hit a pedestrian and I've got to get her to the hospital. She's asking for you."

"Sally," Heather gasped. "Where is she?"

GUESS WHO SHOWS UP NEXT

S + 1 =	G + 1 =	C - 2 =
K - 3 =	A + 4 =	Z - 5 =
A + 0 =	N - 2 =	J + 4 =
W - 3 =	Q - 1 =	W - 3 =
	A + 5 =	I + 0 =
	Z - 5 =	C + 2 =
	H + 4 =	

_ _ _ _   _ _ _ _ _ _ _   _ _ _ _ _ _

CHAPTER 5

At the hospital Sally hopped into the Emergency Room between the pajama-clad Heather and the fashionably dressed woman whose car struck her. Nurses rushed to find a wheelchair as an alert photographer recognized Detective Sally Samuelson, and snapped the unlikely trio's picture. Heather and Sally were shown into a private room, while a policeman pulled the distraught driver to one side.

"How much have you had to drink?" he asked.

"None. Nothing. I haven't been drinking." The driver's hands shook as she searched her handbag for her driver's license. "I understand the woman I hit is a neighbor, but I have no idea what she was doing in my carport at this time of night."

Officer Baker took the petite woman's license. "Tell me exactly what happened."

The woman nervously shifted her handbag from one arm to the other. "I had my parking lights on and was turning into my carport. I suddenly realized someone was crouching there. There was no way I could get stopped fast enough to avoid bumping into her."

The officer continued writing. "You hit Detective Sally Samuelson; a member of the Lewisburg Police Department."

"She's a police officer? I hit a police officer? Oh God! She was probably investigating the burglary that took place at my house last night."

Officer Baker continued, "Let's see if I've got the information right. You're Inez Perkins and you live at number 6-6-3-1 Taborhill Garden Estates. Is that correct?"

Inez nodded, worry lines wrinkling her forehead.

"How fast would you say you were going?"

"We have a ten mile an hour speed limit. I usually go slower than that. As I said, I was pulling into my carport and about to turn the motor off. I didn't expect anyone to be huddled there."

"You were traveling with only your parking lights on?"

"I always switch to parking lights for the short distance between the fire lane and my carport. Neighbors complain when headlights shine in their windows at night."

A door opened and Officer Baker looked up. A doctor walked toward them.

"I'm Dr. Evans," the man in white said. "Are you here about Sally Samuelson?"

Inez nodded. "How is she?"

"She has scrapes and bruises to her upper body, a mild concussion, and a greenstick fracture of her right tibia. She's getting a cast on her leg now."

"Will she be able to go home afterward?" Inez studied the gaunt-faced doctor's sad eyes and generous, pouting lips.

"Even without the break, we'd keep her a day or two. We need to make sure of her cognitive skills before we let her go."

"What do you mean by cognitive skills?" Inez asked.

"We'll make sure she's able to focus her attention and make sense out of what's going on around her. If she can follow geographical directions without being confused, we'll release her."

Officer Baker paused in his note taking. "We sure don't want someone who carries a gun to be confused and unable to focus."

Inez reached out to shake hands with the doctor. "Thank you for taking good care of her."

Doctor Evans shook the woman's hand, suddenly aware of the unusual ring she wore. His grip tightened. "What an interesting piece of jewelry." He pulled her hand toward him to look more closely at the ring. "It's quite unusual. I'll bet it's one of a kind."

Inez quickly pulled her hand back. "Please tell Heather I'll wait for her."

###

"I'm so sorry I injured your sister." Inez and Heather were leaving the hospital. It was still quite dark out. "I'll gladly arrange and finance private nurses if she needs them."

"That shouldn't be necessary," Heather said, as they got in Inez's car. "I'll give our aunt a call and see if she'd like to help." Heather, wearing a hospital bathrobe over her pajamas, shivered.

"Thanks for calling the police when you discovered my home had been broken into yesterday."

"Unfortunately none of your neighbors knew how to contact you."

Inez shrugged. "I think that even if they checked with Doc Adams or Father Raymond, that wouldn't have helped."

Heather nodded. "You're right. I talked to both of them. Neither one knew how to reach you. You should probably leave an emergency number with a trusted friend."

"I'm a courier," Inez explained, turning right at the next boulevard. "Actually, I'm a self-employed independent contractor. The companies I work for send me all over the world to deliver their sensitive material. It's impossible for me to know where I'll be at any given time. What I do to keep in touch is read the local newspaper online. That's how I learned my home had been burglarized."

"You must have been close to Oregon to get here so quickly."

Inez nodded. "I was in Canada this trip. Victoria."

As they entered their housing development Heather said, "Would you like to come in for coffee?"

"Thanks, but I haven't been home since the burglary and I'm anxious to see what happened. I'd like a rain check though."

"You've got it." Heather got out of the car, and waved as she let herself into her empty townhouse. She hurried up the stairs to her office. The guilt she felt weighed heavily. She regretted the accident happening to Sally as she took over responsibilities that weren't hers.

For a while, Heather wished she could avoid asking her aunt to come to Oregon, but Myrtle would be offended if they didn't ask her.

Heather looked from her desk to the narrow bed where design projects lay scattered. Having her aunt visit meant the two of them would share this room. Heather glanced at her watch, figuring the time difference between Oregon and Massachusetts. Reluctantly she dialed her aunt's number.

"Myrtle Wilson." The voice sounded cheerful.

"Hi, Aunt Myrtle. It's Heather. How are you this morning?"

"What's wrong?" Myrtle asked, her voice filled with alarm. "It's 3:00 A.M. in Oregon. You never call this time of day unless it's an emergency. It's Sally, isn't it? Who shot her? Does she have life threatening injuries? Does she need family members to donate blood? No, wait. I'll get the next flight out of Boston. You can count on me for support."

"Stop," shouted Heather. "Wait. It's nothing like that. There was a minor traffic accident. That's all. Sally has a broken leg and a mild concussion."

"That's all?" Myrtle huffed. "She was probably driving a hundred miles an hour, chasing some murderer. Hang up so I can book a flight. I'll call back to let you know what time to expect me in Portland." The line went dead.

Heather sighed, looked at her watch, and hurried to her bedroom to dress. If she didn't go to bed and skipped either breakfast or lunch, she might get the Coffman Jewelers website finished before the drive to Portland International.

###

The day flew by. Too quickly it was time to go to Portland to pick up Aunt Myrtle. Heather had done all she could to finish the Coffman Jewelers website without consulting her client. For an hour she'd been calling motels near the Delaware capital, trying to find where her mom had made a reservation. Number seven on the list had just started ringing.

"Travelers Best," answered a cheerful voice.

"My name is Heather Samuelson and I'm checking on a reservation my mom made." Heather intended to skate close enough to the truth to get the information she needed. "Mom is getting forgetful. The reservation number she wrote down for September 15 is N9RT7G. She needs a non-smoking room and she's afraid she forgot to ask for one."

"N9RT7G? That's a non-smoking double for Ella Prince."

Heather smiled at the name her mom had used. "Thank goodness; she will be so relieved."

Heather hung up. She'd located her mother's secret meeting place, and if she had requested two beds, then she was definitely expecting company.

"I thought that plane would never get here," Myrtle complained. The flamboyant woman in her middle fifties wore a startling purple dress.

"You were lucky to change planes only once and arrive so soon." Heather studied her mother's identical twin. The graying hair over reading glasses that clung to the end of her nose looked so much like her mother that for a minute, Heather could hardly breathe.

"Well, let's get going," Myrtle said, ignoring her niece's inspection.

Heather picked up a small cosmetic case and grabbed the handle of a large suitcase.

"How's Sally doing?" Myrtle asked as they walked toward the parking garage.

"I stopped to see her before I left town. She has a headache and her leg is in a cast. Her biggest complaint at the moment is that she hates bedpans."

Myrtle nodded. "I don't blame her. Do you still have neighbors pushing baked goods off on you girls? Any more coconut cakes I can help eat?"

"We have empty townhouses on both sides of ours. The Bender sisters moved into assisted living and Helen Corbin married one of Sally's coworkers. She and her boys moved to his place. They're selling Helen's."

"We should have lots of quiet time then. While we drive, bring me up-to-date with what's going on in your life and then go into detail on how Sally ended up with a fracture and a concussion."

"And that's the whole story," Heather said two hours later.

"Whoa! Some babe in a big black car, traveling without headlights, smashes into my niece and she's not even cited for reckless driving?" Myrtle's eyes widened. "I hope Sally sues the pants off that broad."

Heather slowed to ten miles per hour as they pulled into TGE.

"I'll never get used to you girls living here." Myrtle eyed the collection of sixty, two-story townhouses she'd visited in July.

Heather pulled into her carport. "Oh, good. The newspaper's here." She glanced at her aunt. "Why don't you get the paper while I bring in the suitcases?" She set the brake and got out of the car to unload the suitcases.

Myrtle hurried to the front porch and grabbed the newspaper. She began unrolling it. "Oh, oh! You made the front page."

"I did what?" Heather dropped the suitcases.

"Take a look." Myrtle thrust the newspaper at Heather.

The picture on the *Clarion*'s front page showed pajama-clad Heather supporting a disheveled Sally on her right, while Inez Perkins, on Sally's left, looked like she'd stepped from the pages of a fashion magazine. The women's faces were shadowed.

The headline read: *Samuelson Curse Strikes Again*. The accompanying story detailed Charlie Samuelson's death on Mt. Hood and his wife's drowning when her car ended up in February's flood waters.

"I wonder if Sally's seen this." Heather glanced at her aunt. "How hungry are you?"

"If the real question is *do I want to see Sally right this minute*, then the answer is *yes*. Put the suitcases in the house and let's go." Myrtle stepped from the porch, then turned. "Well, what's taking you so long?" She waited, hands on her hips.

Heather shook her head, unlocked the door, and set suitcases inside. She locked the door and silently followed her aunt back to the car.

Laughter filled the room as another of the Clarion's subscribers looked up from the newspaper and dialed the phone. "Did you see the paper today? We might have that window of opportunity we need to get a few 'bugs' installed in the Samuelson house."

"I saw it. With everyone at the hospital consoling the cop with the broken leg, the house should be empty long enough for me to do the job."

"I'm betting we'll soon know if things are as they seem or if someone is playing fast and loose with us."

###

"What did you learn about Bishop's appeals?" Jazz waited for Ox to answer.

"His attorney is still filing them, but his options are almost exhausted." Ox shuffled papers on his desk.

Jazz had seen them all and knew there was nothing new to consider. "I suppose we aren't any closer to identifying Bishop's hit man?"

"Not that I know of," Ox sighed. "Actually we aren't any closer to proving the deaths of all those people connected to Bishop's trials were murders and not accidents."

"Whoever Bishop hired to do his dirty work is careful and slick. He's been polishing off people since the day the trial ended eight years ago."

Ox laughed. "The assassin's so good no one except you and I suspect he even exists."

A SEARCH GETS UNDERWAY

Find the little word that fits within the bigger word.
Use each little word only once.

AIL, BAT, EVE, HAD, ONE, RAG, RAT, TAN

D _ _ _ O N   S _ _ _ D   M _ _ _ Y   P R O _ _ _ I O N

S _ _ _ E S   N _ _ _ R   J _ _ _ S   O P E _ _ _ I O N

CHAPTER 6

"I saw it," grumped Sally. A copy of the *Clarion* lay at the foot of her bed.

"Your poor face, and your arms," Myrtle moaned, reaching out to gingerly pat her niece.

"Enough, Aunt Myrtle. Don't touch me; I hurt everywhere."

"Complain, complain." The comments came from the man in the doorway of Sally's private room.

"It's the kid doctor again," Sally said, referring to the man twice her age who had been her physician for two decades. "If I do enough complaining, you might let me go home now that my auntie can take care of me."

"That does make getting you out of here more attractive." The doctor checked Sally's pulse and planted his cold stethoscope against her chest.

"Aunt Myrtle, this is Dr. Weston Evans, a heartless individual if there ever was one."

Dr. Evans nodded at Myrtle. "You must be the aunt I've heard so much about over the years. I'm glad to finally meet you, Myrtle. You sure look like your sister, Matilda."

"So I've been told," Myrtle replied. "When can Sally come home?"

Dr. Evans turned to his patient. "I'm not sure one overnight is enough. What I am sure of is that spending just these last few hours here is definitely *not* sufficient." He turned to Sally. "If you'll settle down and be a good patient, we'll consider sending you home tomorrow." He checked her eyes. "How's your memory? Do you recall the accident?"

"I remember dropping the map." Sally frowned. "Heather's flashlight had quit so it was dark. I couldn't see the map on the ground. My cell phone started ringing, so I stood up to get it out of my pocket. I think

I bent down to continue looking for the map—just before something pushed me to the ground."

"Not bad," Dr. Evans said. "Can you tell me how to get from the hospital to your home?"

Sally frowned. "Recalling street names hurts, but I think I could find my way."

"Ladies," Dr. Evans said, "We need to let our patient get more rest. Check back in the morning and I'll let you know how soon to expect her home."

"I *told* you he was heartless." Sally snuggled down in her puddle of covers.

"Has Inez Perkins been in to see you?" Dr. Evans asked. "Usually the person who causes an accident haunts a patient's bedside."

"She's called," Sally responded, yawning, "dozens of times."

Heather added, "Her house was burglarized recently. She's got some insurance problems in addition to her concern for Sally."

"Whoa! It sounds to me like the Samuelson Curse the *Clarion* spoke of has spawned the Perkins Curse—a robbery *and* a car accident? Within hours of each other? We'll get Sally out of here as soon as we can. This curse-thing might be contagious." Dr. Evans turned and hurried from the room humming *London Bridge is Falling Down*.

"Watch your step," Heather cautioned as she and Myrtle got out of the car back at the townhouse. They'd checked on Sally to their satisfaction and it was now well past dinnertime. Heather pointed to puddles of water. "It looks like there's been another rain storm while we were at the hospital."

Myrtle stepped around a puddle near the front porch. "Hurry up and unlock the door. I can hardly wait to get unpacked."

Heather pulled the house key from her pocket, and pushed it in the lock. The door immediately swung open. "That's strange. It looks like I forgot to lock up when we left." She put the key back in her purse.

"But you didn't forget," Myrtle whispered. "I watched you lock the door."

"One of us is getting forgetful." Heather politely stepped aside so Myrtle could enter.

Myrtle took one step forward, then stopped. She whispered, "You'd better check this out."

"What are you talking about?"

Myrtle pointed. "I think those are footprints on your nice new carpeting."

Heather looked past her aunt. Sure enough, damp shoes had recently moved across the carpet, from the door to the stairs. Heather stepped back. "Get in the car," she whispered, tugging on Myrtle's arm. "The intruder may still be in there. I'm getting us some help." She pulled out her cell phone and hit the speed dial for Jazz.

"What's going on," he asked when he arrived.

Heather and Myrtle got out of the car, each of them trying to answer his question.

"Hold on," he said, moving to the door to look in the house. "I don't see any wet footprints."

"Then they dried. But I'm telling you, someone broke in while we were at the hospital checking on Sally. They even unlocked the door."

Gun drawn, Jazz stepped quietly into the house, touring the first floor rooms. In a moment he was back at the front door where Heather and Myrtle waited. He whispered, "Stay back. The first floor is safe; I'll check upstairs." He climbed the carpeted stairs while the two women fidgeted at the front door. "It's clear," he called, coming back down. "It looks like whoever was here has gone."

The women cautiously entered. "Did you check the closets?" Myrtle asked.

Jazz nodded, smiling. "And under the beds."

Heather whispered, "Are things pulled from drawers?"

"Actually, nothing looks disturbed. Check it out for yourself. It doesn't look like anyone went through your things."

Heather stepped into the house and hurried to her office. "You're right," she said in a hushed voice, returning downstairs. "Other than the unlocked door and those footprints, there's no sign anyone was here. What was the intruder looking for, I wonder?"

"Cash, probably. Why are you whispering?"

"I feel like someone's looking over my shoulder." She shivered. In a normal voice she added, "I don't see any sign of an intruder being here, and that doesn't make sense."

"Maybe he inventoried things he wants to carry out later. I suggest you install an alarm system as soon as possible."

"Where've you been," Ox asked when Jazz returned to the office. "The lieutenant was looking for you."

"Heather had an emergency. Someone broke into her house and she thought the intruder might still be inside."

"Anything taken?"

"Nothing that was obvious. If it was anyone other than Heather telling me about vanishing footprints, I wouldn't believe them."

"Footprints, huh? That's a pretty careless burglar."

Jazz nodded and began writing in his notebook.

The sun wasn't up when the doorbell at the Samuelson's rang the next morning. Heather climbed from bed, put on a robe and made her way downstairs. She yawned as she opened the front door.

"Heather, I'm sorry to be so early, but I have to leave in a few hours. I wanted to check on Sally first, but the hospital won't tell me a thing." Inez Perkins had dark circles under her eyes. Thin, gray hair matted her forehead. She wore jeans and a flannel shirt of vivid reds and greens. A manila envelope was tucked under one arm.

"Come in, Inez. I'll start the coffee. We could both use something to perk us up."

"Thank you. That would be wonderful." Inez followed Heather to the kitchen. "How's your sister doing? Not only won't the hospital tell me anything, but half the time they won't put me through to her room."

"My aunt and I saw her last night." Heather started the coffee and motioned to the dining room table.

Inez slumped in one of the chairs. "Is she feeling better?"

"She's complaining about bedpans. I took that to mean she'll be her old self in a day or two."

"Did her doctor say when she could come home?" Inez pushed hair from her eyes, twisting it to loop behind one ear.

"We're to check later this morning. Do you take cream or sugar?"

"Black, please."

"You said you were leaving. Where to this time?" Heather put coffee mugs on the table as perking sounds began.

"I'm headed for Taiwan. An investment bank wants documents handed over to one of their budding geniuses tomorrow. It'll take me about eighteen hours to get there."

"They certainly don't give you much time between assignments." Heather reached for the coffee pot and filled their mugs.

"I have the burglary and cleanup under control. The security service has my alarm working again, and I've given a list of what's missing to the insurance company and the police. It's Sally I haven't dealt with to my satisfaction."

"She'll be fine," Heather assured her, settling in a chair across from her neighbor. "What did the burglars take?"

"Some personal trinkets are missing, but nothing irreplaceable or of great value. They took some documents, valueless except for use in identity theft, and they damaged a few things. I've cancelled all my credit cards."

Inez looked first at the envelope in her lap, then at Heather. "I have a favor to ask. Because my job takes me out of the country, I don't have close friends in town. I need to leave a house key with someone so repairs to my hutch can be made late this afternoon. I'll be gone before the workman arrives. Would you . . . ?" She paused, pushing a tagged key across the table.

"Of course. I'd be glad to help." Heather reached for the key.

"Thanks. I'll rest easier knowing you're backing me up. The code for my alarm system is on the tag." Inez stared solemnly into Heather's eyes. "I know I can trust you girls."

Heather blinked and smiled. "It's kind of you to say that, but you don't really know anything about us."

Inez laughed and flushed. "Actually I do. In view of Sally's injuries, I checked you out pretty thoroughly. I felt like I needed to know something about you."

"That's sensible," Heather said.

"Being in charge of my house key isn't the only favor I'd like to ask." Inez paused, nervously turning the sealed envelope end to end. "I'd like to leave this with you. My house has been broken into twice in the last few months. I need to get these documents out of there."

"Someone must know when you're gone. Why don't you put your documents in a safety deposit box?"

Inez pushed the envelope across the table. "Because of my job I try to avoid getting my name on things that can be used to help people find me. Kidnapping couriers happens oftener than you might guess. Please hold on to this until I ask for it." She smiled and added, "Or until I drop dead—whichever comes first!"

Before Heather could respond they heard a gasp.

"Kiki?" The empty coffee cup Myrtle had been carrying downstairs dropped to the floor and shattered.

Heather jumped to her feet. "I'll get it." She hurried to find a broom and dust pan.

Myrtle seemed not to notice the broken cup. "Is it really you, Kiki?" She entered the dining room still in her pajamas and bathrobe, staring at Inez.

"I beg your pardon?" Inez focused a puzzled smile, first on Myrtle, then on Heather.

"Aunt Myrtle," Heather said, "this is our neighbor, Inez Perkins. Inez, this is my aunt, Myrtle Wilson. She flew out from Boston yesterday to help take care of Sally."

Inez reached out to shake Myrtle's hand. "It's nice meeting you, although I'm sorry about the reason you had to come west."

"You look so much like someone I used to know," Myrtle said, studying the face of Heather's neighbor. "Her name was Kiki Kelly— Kathleen, really. She was a year or two ahead of me in school in Hudson, Massachusetts. We were good friends, but then she graduated and moved." Myrtle cleared her throat. "We were kids together, pledging we'd stay single for life or we'd become famous." She laughed. "Not both. Obviously I settled for staying single since I haven't managed to become famous."

Inez said, "You still have time, you know. I'm assuming you didn't keep in touch with your friend?"

"I didn't know how. She didn't leave a forwarding address when she graduated. I'm sorry you aren't her. It would mean so much to me to find her after all these years."

The doorbell rang and Heather hurried to admit two chattering nephews and their mom.

"Aunt Heather," exclaimed one of the twins. It was becoming difficult to tell Tim from Tom. "We got to see Aunt Sally's neat cast."

"Hi, Heather." Rachel sounded tired. She gave her sons a gentle nudge to get them inside the door. "We got an early start today and when I saw your lights were on, we decided we had time to stop in and give Aunt Myrtle a welcoming hug."

"Hi, Great-Aunt Myrtle," the boys greeted in unison. "You didn't sign Sally's cast yet."

Myrtle reached out to enclose her niece in a cloud of perfume and welcoming arms, then turned to the boys. "Your turn." She bent down to the ten-year-olds. "I'll sign the cast later, if you've left me any room."

"Oh, you have company." Rachel noticed Heather's guest for the first time. "We shouldn't have stopped." She put a hand on each of her sons. "We'll come back later."

Heather gestured toward Inez. "It's okay, Rachel. This is my neighbor, Inez Perkins. Inez, this is my sister Rachel Bennett and her sons, Tim and Tom."

"It's nice meeting the middle sister," Inez laughed, reaching out to shake hands. "Your sons are quite handsome." She studied their faces, then looked back at Rachel. "You're so lucky to have them." Inez turned to Heather, "I need to head home and pack. If you go to the hospital later this morning, I'd like to go with you."

Heather nodded. "We'll phone when we're ready."

"Let me give you a number." Inez fished in a pocket for a business card. "This is my cell phone number. It will reach me nearly any time of the day or night, wherever I am. But," she hesitated, "I'd prefer you didn't use it unless there's an absolute emergency. The number penciled on the back is the one to use. You can leave a message."

Heather nodded and took the card. After Inez left, she returned to the kitchen, her forehead knotted in frowns.

"Rachel volunteered to help with Sally," Aunt Myrtle said. "It sounds to me like I can pack up and go home."

"Not so fast, Auntie," laughed Rachel. "I have some news."

Heather motioned Rachel in the direction of the coffee pot. "Help yourself." A thoughtful expression remained on her face.

"Are you all right, Heather?" Myrtle could see something was troubling her niece.

"We get to go with Dad on his next trip," shouted one of the twins, interrupting the conversation.

Rachel laughed. "Leave it to the boys. That's our news. Jason has to go to Washington, D. C. We've decided to take the boys and do some touring. We leave in a week and will be gone seven days."

"Wow, forget about lending a hand here." Myrtle looked at the weary expression on Rachel's face. "I'm glad it isn't me."

"You'll have fun," Heather murmured in a distracted way. Then she said, "Wait! I know what was different!"

"What are you talking about?" asked Rachel.

"The other night at the hospital Inez had thick, white hair. This morning, it's thin and gray."

"She looked like she hadn't rested very well," Myrtle added. "Maybe she wore a wig at the time of the accident."

"Today she looks like someone on chemotherapy. Could that be possible?" Heather was thinking about the instructions she'd received with the sealed envelope regarding holding it until Inez asked for it or dropped dead. Those instructions made sense if Inez was battling cancer.

"Was that the lady who hit Sally?" Rachel asked.

"It was." Heather picked up the manila envelope, the business card, and the key Inez had given her. "I'll be back as soon as I put these away." She headed up the stairs, wondering about a key she could feel inside the sealed envelope. She slipped the items into her Coffman Jewelers folder because it was handy, and then she paused.

Inez had known instantly that Rachel was the middle sister. What kind of checking on them had she been doing?

###

WHAT'S GOING ON NOW?

Add a letter to each word below to form a new word.
The addition may be at the beginning, end, or within the word.
Place the added letter on the line below the boxes to form
an 8-letter and 4-letter word answering the question.

C E I K L O P R R T T Y

race	bide	lad	one	new	very	spot	ear
trace							

___T_____

sort	pan	curt	ail
sport			

___P_____

CHAPTER 7

"Let's get our invalid home," Heather said, nodding at Myrtle and Inez as they entered the hospital.

"My thoughts exactly," Inez replied. She wore the same flannel shirt and jeans she had worn earlier that morning, but her graying hair was again snow white.

"Hi, Sally." Heather hurried into her sister's room. "I brought a crew along to help get you home. Are you ready to go?"

Myrtle walked to the far side of the bed and picked up a bouquet. "I'll carry the flowers," she said.

Sally shook her head. "Dr. Evans is still doing paper work. The release process is going slower than expected."

Myrtle held up the card accompanying the large bouquet of white daisies and blue bachelor buttons. "Is this from an admirer you haven't told us about?"

"Read the card." Sally shifted her position to look at Heather.

"*Get well, Supercilious Sally,*" Aunt Myrtle read. "*You are loved.*"

"Oh." The sound escaped before Heather could control it. Tears filled her eyes.

Myrtle looked up. "It sounds to me like a boyfriend."

"Does it?" Sally studied Heather's face.

"I . . . I got a little catch in my throat," Heather whispered, clearing her throat. She dabbed at her wet eyes. "May I see the card, Aunt Myrtle?" When it exchanged hands, Heather said, "I didn't know anyone called you *Supercilious Sally* anymore."

"No one does. At least, not that I'm aware of. In fact I haven't heard that expression for eight or nine years."

Heather nodded her understanding. It was a pet name their dad had used.

"The card's unsigned," Myrtle said. "Whoever sent it used the same florist who delivered that unsigned arrangement to my sister's memorial service."

"Ah ha!" The comment came from the doorway. "I see everyone is here except the Lewisburg Police Department and your nephews." Dr. Evans stepped into the room.

Sally explained, "Rachel and the twins were here this morning, Dr. Evans. You missed them. Look what the boys did to my cast." She pulled her blanket aside to display the decorations.

Heather said, "They stopped to see Myrtle before school this morning. I thought Rachel looked tired."

"It's those boys," Myrtle said. "They'd tire anyone."

"Dr. Evans?" Inez interrupted. "Is Sally ready to leave?"

"Almost. We're letting her go because we're short of beds, and it seems to make people nervous having a lot of cops wandering around the halls."

"Half of my department dropped in this morning," Sally explained with a smile.

Dr. Evans turned to Inez. "We should have the paper work done soon, then we'll prescribe meds, arrange checkup times, and fit her for crutches. I expect she'll be ready to leave by late afternoon."

"Afternoon?" Inez wore a startled expression.

"Sorry. That's the best we can do." He checked the size of Sally's pupils. "When she gets home, she's not to put any weight on that foot for a couple of days. The break will take six to eight weeks to heal."

"Six weeks?" Sally gulped.

"Or eight," Dr. Evans reminded her. He turned to Inez, "I'd like to talk to you, please, Ms. Perkins." He motioned for her to follow him as he left the room humming softly under his breath. In the hallway he turned to wait for her.

Heather had expected to be consulted concerning Sally's accident. Curious to know if the doctor would bring up insurance matters with Inez, Heather moved closer to the open doorway to listen.

###

"I hope you'll excuse my curiosity," Dr. Evans was saying, "but I'd like to know more about that interesting ring you wore yesterday. I'm guessing it was fourteen karat two-tone gold with two carats total weight in diamonds."

"That's it exactly." Inez sounded surprised. "It's one of my favorites. I picked it up in Turkey, at a little shop I'll probably never find again. I've often wished I'd bought a few more things there since they did such marvelous detail work."

"Turkey? I was hoping you'd say you got it stateside at a jewelry store, or maybe a pawn shop."

"Pawn shop? I don't buy things from pawn shops. Why is it important for you to know about my ring?"

He sighed. "It's one of those sad stories people are either reluctant to tell or eager to tell every chance they get. The description I mentioned matches the classic marquise three stone ring I was having designed for my fiancé who, it turned out, was very superstitious. When the ring was stolen from the jeweler designing it, she took it as a bad omen and decided not to marry me."

"My God! A ring similar to mine changed your entire life?"

"Is there any chance you'd consider selling your ring to me?"

"I'll give it some thought," Inez said, "but it's one of my favorites and can't be replaced."

"I'd appreciate it, if you'd check for an inscription engraved in it."

"An inscription? I've never noticed one."

"Do me the favor of looking. It might read, '*W+ME 4ever.*' That's *Weston and Mary Ellen forever.*" He gave an abrupt laugh. "Obviously our forever didn't even get off the ground."

"You think someone stole your ring and sold it in Turkey?" Inez studied the doctor's face, then she asked, "What happened to your superstitious fiancé?"

"I had waited a long time for Mary Ellen to show up in my life. After the ring was stolen and time passed, she became Mrs. Gerald Hansen and moved away."

"But you kept in touch?"

"Not until Gerald died two years ago. I stayed out of her life. After meeting you yesterday, and seeing that ring, it occurs to me that if I found a similar ring after all these years, my superstitious sweetheart might return to me just like the ring."

"How exactly are we going to deal with Babe if there's a screw-up?"

"There won't be a screw up. She's going to come to me. I've already baited the trap in case our other arrangements for her don't work out."

"If she comes to you, then what?"

"Then, with my fingers wrapped around her throat, I'm going to punish her for all the grief she's caused you and me over the years."

"Babe is so slick your bait will be gone from the trap before you know she's even been close to it."

"I'm preparing for that eventuality. If she so much as handles the bait, she's a dead woman."

Back at Taborhill, Inez got out of Heather's car. "I won't be around when they finally let Sally go."

"We'll manage," Heather assured her, wondering why her usually bubbly aunt was saying so little.

"I had this cashier's check made out to you." Inez handed the check to Heather. "If it doesn't cover expenses, I'll take care of that when I get home again."

"When do you expect to return?" Heather accepted the check, noting the generous amount.

"Within a week, although it may be as long as ten days. Usually my next assignment reaches me while I'm making a delivery, so my return isn't always predictable."

"How can they do that?"

"They contact the place where I make my delivery, by cell phone if there's cell phone service, otherwise by two-way radio or telegram. They'll tell me where to pick up the next item, usually at another location in whatever city I'm already in. I'll pick it up, and then I'm off to a new location."

"I wouldn't like a job like that," Heather said. "You can't plan ahead."

"It's perfect for a single woman with no family, who likes seeing the world. Sorry to dash off, but I have to finish packing." She waved and hurried home.

"Why so quiet, Aunt Myrt?" Heather asked as they stepped indoors. "Aren't you feeling well?"

"I'll tell you why I'm quiet, Heather Samuelson." Myrtle whirled to face her niece, fists thrust against her hips. "I don't care what that woman says. She's Kiki Kelly. That's why I'm quiet. I keep wondering why she's denying it. Why she won't admit she knows me?" Myrtle paused a moment, breathing hard. "Doesn't she want to know me anymore?" Myrtle's frustration slowly drained away, replaced by sadness. "We could be having such good times together. And if her use of wigs represents chemotherapy, then I could be taking care of her." She turned and sank down on the sofa.

"What makes you so sure she's Kiki Kelly?" Heather asked.

"There's a string of small moles just under her left ear; six of them, as I recall. It's Kiki all right."

"I didn't notice any moles."

"They are light-colored, and covered with makeup. But they were there. Her high collar smudged the makeup so the moles are beginning to show through. Check her neck the next time you see her." Myrtle looked like she wanted to cry.

"It's as good as done!" Heather grabbed a piece of paper, scribbled a message, and picked up a roll of tape. "I'll be right back." She dashed out the door.

At 6631 Inez's car was still in the carport. Heather rang the doorbell and waited.

"Did I forget something?" Inez asked when she came to the door. Her suitcase was at her side.

"I brought a note for the glazier. I'll tape it to your door so he'll know where to pick up a key." Heather tore off a piece of tape and attached the note to the door frame, forcing Inez to look to her right to read it. The action exposed the left side of her neck. Sure enough, six moles could be seen under her left ear.

Inez read Heather's note: *Glazier: key at 6673.* "I already gave him that information over the phone, but I suppose a note is good backup."

"See you when you get back." Heather waved, ready to walk home.

Inez picked up her suitcase and turned on her alarm. She stepped out and locked the door. "Would you do another favor for me? Check with Brad to see if he can get that street light near my house to stay on at night." Inez pointed to the light that Aba Brothers Electrical had recently worked on.

"I'll see what we can do," Heather said.

There were questions about Inez that needed answering and Heather planned to get started on them immediately. She wanted to know why her neighbor pretended not to know Myrtle Wilson.

Heather checked her watch. Coffman Jewelers, the new website jewelry mogul, would have to wait for the changes Abe wanted on his website. There were more pressing puzzles to be solved.

###

SOMEONE NEEDS SYMPATHY

M + 3 =	A + 3 =	A + 4 =
L + 3 =	P + 2 =	P + 6 =
R - 3 =		F - 5 =
V - 4 =		Q - 3 =
		M + 6 =

<u>P</u> _ _ _ _ _ _ _ _ _ _

CHAPTER 8

"Want to go for a ride?" Heather looked at her watch as she cleared the table. "The hospital gave me a time to pick Sally up, but it's still too early."

"What do you have in mind?" Myrtle continued stacking things in the dishwasher.

"I thought we might talk to Father Adams about his dad's background. If Doc Adams lived near the town where you grew up, you might have known him."

"Didn't you tell me he was in his eighties? How old do you think I am?" Myrtle tried to look insulted and failed.

Heather laughed. "My hunch is that if Kiki and you are from the Hudson area of Massachusetts, then . . . ."

"Got it!" Myrtle agreed, beaming at her niece. "If Doc Adams lived there, it would answer some of our questions."

Heather nodded. "If he's from the Hudson area, we'll have common threads to begin checking for other details."

"We can pick Sally up after seeing Doc and his son," Myrtle said.

"My thoughts exactly," Heather agreed. "Grab your purse and let's go. I've got one short errand to run first."

At United Florists, Heather dashed in with the unsigned card from Sally's flowers. "Sorry to trouble you." She handed the card to the clerk. "Is there any way you can tell me who sent flowers to Sally Samuelson at Good Samaritan?"

The clerk looked at the card and then at his delivery records. "It was a cash purchase," he explained. "We don't keep records of who makes cash purchases."

"Just like before." Heather rejoined Myrtle in the car. "Whoever purchased Sally's flowers didn't want to be identified. I don't mind our family having a mysterious friend, but I'd like to know how that friend knows intimate details, like pet names for both Mom and Sally."

"We wanted you to know your father's renter surfaced briefly." Heather and Myrtle had stopped to see Father Adams at St. Mary's.

"I saw the picture in the *Clarion* and recognized the name. I tried calling her, but she has an unlisted number. Luckily she called me this morning. I'd like to have met her but she's gone again."

"Father Adams, did your dad ever live on the East Coast? Anywhere near Boston?" Myrtle waited, hardly breathing.

"As a matter of fact, Dad lived in Hudson, but that was about thirty years ago." Father Adams's fixed smile spread across his face.

"I knew it," Myrtle sighed. "I'm from Hudson. I bet I knew your dad." She smiled coyly. "He was probably my babysitter."

"I suppose he could have been, although it's more likely he entertained at one of your birthday parties. He liked to do magic tricks and got pretty good at them. It was a hobby he pursued for years."

"Was he living in Hudson when Inez approached him about the house?" Heather asked.

"Not to my knowledge, although that might have been their connection. I believe I told you that he's owned that house for more than thirty years."

"What was your dad's occupation when he was a young man?" Myrtle asked. "I think the Doc Adams I knew was a teacher of some kind."

"Dad has always been good with his hands and as I said, he liked to impress people with magic tricks. Sleight-of-hand. He was a court stenographer for years. When he moved from the East Coast he opened a school for magicians. It was a place where those interested in magic could go to practice and perform their tricks in an intimate setting. If they had good hands, they earned the right to move on to advanced techniques and training. Dad said they'd find magic was a 'portal to wealth.' Of course it didn't turn out that way for him. Eventually I was able to transfer to this area because Dad was getting old enough that he needed help. I think it's just a fluke that the house Inez bought is also here."

"It's kind of you to let us take your time," Myrtle said. "I'll have to give more thought to magicians who entertained at parties. It's fun to find friends one hasn't seen in a long time. What's your dad's given name?"

"He's Harold Adams. You should ask him your questions. His mind is pretty sharp if you catch him at a time when he's willing to talk." Father Adams grinned. "I've just remembered that Dad claimed only mediocre magicians used *abracadabra* for magic incantations. He used *hickory dickory dock*. That's where he picked up the nickname, Doc."

"It sounds to me like he was quite an original thinker."

"That he was. You ladies stop in any time. Thanks for making sure I knew Inez had surfaced."

Heather moved toward the door. "By the way, have you ever heard the name Kiki Kelly or Kathleen Kelly?"

Father Adams shook his head. "Can't say it's familiar. Is she local?"

"She used to live in Hudson with Myrtle."

"Sorry. That name isn't familiar."

Outside the church, Heather said, "The Boardwalk Nursing Home isn't far. Want to go?"

"You bet. We need to start getting our questions answered."

"We'll stop at a grocery and get some peppermints to take along."

"Peppermints?"

"You'll see."

###

"Look who's back, Doc," called Jake Lundeen when Heather and Myrtle walked into room 465. He lowered his voice, "Got any pills on you this trip, Babe?"

"Shhh!" Heather cautioned, opening a bag to allow him to reach in.

He grabbed the entire bag of mints. "You can bring Doc some on your next trip. This isn't his kind, but it's my kind." He fumbled with the paper, then popped a mint in his mouth.

Heather walked to the second bed where Doc Adams lay. "Hello, Doc," she said. "This is my Aunt Myrtle Wilson. She's from Hudson the same as you and Kiki."

The women watched Doc, eager for his reply and reaction.

"Saw her yesterday," he said with a brief nod. "Nice lady. Got good hands."

"Did you meet Kiki in Hudson," Myrtle asked, winking at her niece.

"My best student," he whispered. "Has good hands." He raised arthritic fingers, then let them drop on the bed.

"Did she attend your magician's school? Is that where you met her?"

Doc Adams laughed, lifted his knobby fingers once more and wiggled them in the air. "Hocus pocus," he whispered. "Taught her hocus pocus. Need good hands for that." He gave his own appendages a disappointed look and tucked them under the covers.

"How did you meet Kiki?" Myrtle asked.

Doc Adams closed his eyes. "Can't call her that. Gotta new name." In a moment he began snoring softly, with little bubbling sounds.

The women slowly moved away from his bed, heading for the door.

"Got any more pills?" Jake asked as they approached. "You bring me more pills and come back tomorrow. I'll tell you what Doc said to that lady you're asking about."

"Thanks, Jake," Heather said. "We'd like that. See you tomorrow." She and Myrtle walked down the hall, comparing notes. "Not only didn't Doc question the name Kiki, but he said he taught her magic tricks, and hocus pocus. I wonder what he meant by that?"

Myrtle laughed. "Kiki already had more than a few tricks up her sleeve."

"When she comes back, we'll let her entertain us." Heather smiled. "Now then, let's get Sally home."

###

BEFORE AND AFTER

How's the brain doing? Does it need a little exercise? Okay, let's exercise it. Find a word that joins with the words before and after the blank line. For instance: LOVE _____ EGG needs NEST to form love nest and nest egg.

BEAR, BODY, FIRE, GUN, HERRING, KNIFE,
MONEY, PRINCE, SHIP, TAIL

BUTTER	_____	WOUND
BLACK	_____	CUB
DEAD	_____	BAG
FLAG	_____	BOARD
FROG	_____	CHARMING
FUNNY	_____	CLIP
HOUSE	_____	ENGINE
PUPPY	_____	END
RED	_____	BONE
SHOT	_____	SHOT

CHAPTER 9

The man hired to replace the glass doors in Inez's hutch was waiting when Heather and Aunt Myrtle arrived home with Sally. After they put her to bed, Heather got the key and alarm code for Inez's house and moments later disarmed her neighbor's newly repaired alarm system.

"Nice place," the repairman said as he and Heather walked through the living room. "This job won't take long. Will you be sticking around?"

Heather nodded; she'd noticed a framed photograph of a young boy with blond hair. *No family to be considered?* Wasn't that what Inez had said when she explained her career choice? Thoughtfully, Heather followed the repairman to the hutch with broken glass. A sealed envelope with his name on it leaned against a shelf. He checked the contents, then tucked the envelope in his pocket.

"Nice lady. She said she'd leave my money here." He patted his pocket and started work on replacing the hutch's glass doors.

Heather watched, still wondering about the young boy's picture. Why was her aunt's friend pretending she wasn't who she really was? And if she had no family, who was the child in the picture? At that moment, a shrill sound pierced the silence. After several more shrill rings, the phone's recording feature turned on.

"I bet you thought having an unlisted number would keep you from getting the phone call you've been dreading for decades," a man said. *"Think of me and this call when you wake in the middle of the night, because the past has caught up with you. You are a cicatrix on society and you will be excised."* The caller hung up.

A shiver crawled up Heather's back.

"What the hell is a *seek-a-tricks*?" the repairman asked, pausing in his work. "That sounded like a threat."

"I feel like we've been eavesdropping." Heather looked at the flashing message light. "Finish up and let's get out of here."

"I just need to make sure these doors slide like they're supposed to." He tested the doors. "Maybe we should notify Ms. Perkins about that threat?"

"I'll take care of it," Heather said.

The repairman nodded and picked up his tools. As they left, Heather turned on the alarm and locked the door, then hurried to her car. If burglars saw a car in Inez's carport, they might stay away. Heather moved her van there, then rushed home to put the key and alarm code for Inez's house in a folder with her neighbor's other items.

"We're in here," called Myrtle, from Sally's room. "Everything's under control."

Heather took Inez's business card from the folder and joined her aunt in Sally's room. At her sister's side was a stack of new magazines. "Jazz stopped by with reading material," laughed Sally.

"Did you get Inez's hutch repaired?" Myrtle asked.

Heather nodded. "Do either of you know the meaning of the word cicatrix?"

"Use it in a sentence," Sally said.

Heather repeated the caller's message.

"Where's a dictionary?" Myrtle asked.

Sally pointed to her bookshelf, and Myrtle grabbed the dictionary, paging through it as she mumbled, *seek-a-tricks*.

"Why would anyone threaten Inez?" Sally asked. "Do you think she's injured other people with her driving?"

"The threat mentioned her past catching up with her, so I'm guessing it has to be something from years ago. Because she's using an alias, we need to make sure she isn't wanted by the police."

Myrtle shut the dictionary with a loud thump and set it aside. "The dictionary says a cicatrix is a scar, a blemish. It's a medical term."

"Then someone thinks Inez is a blemish on society." Heather shivered. "It sounded to me like a threat when the caller said she'd be excised."

Sally nodded. "I agree. It's definitely a threat."

"Another thing puzzles me," Heather said. "There's a picture of a young boy in her living room."

"I remember seeing that," Sally said, "when I did a walk-through after her robbery."

Myrtle interrupted. "But Inez told us she didn't have any family. When I knew her, her parents were dead and she didn't have other relatives. It's one of the reasons we became close friends. My parents were dead, and I only had my sister."

"That means the young boy in the picture can't be a nephew," Heather reasoned. "Of course he could be the son of a friend."

"If Inez married," Myrtle said, "that might account for the name change, but it doesn't account for why she's denying she's Kathleen Kelly."

"If the young boy is her son, I wonder how old he is now, and where he is. We need to know more about our neighbor. I'll check on the internet. Maybe that will tell us why someone's threatening her." Heather glanced at Sally. "Can you make sure she's not a fugitive?"

"My lieutenant is bringing a new at-home cop computer to me," Sally said. "It's loaded with law enforcement programs. I might be able to use it to see her status."

Heather studied the business card she'd pulled from the folder with Inez's things. "You check on that, and I'll visit Worldwide Courier and Delivery Service to see if they'll tell me anything about their employee."

Myrtle said, "I've been recalling wild times Kiki and I shared."

"How wild?" Heather asked, hugging her aunt.

"Maybe not wild by today's standards," Myrtle explained. "But wild for the world I grew up in." She laughed. "We saw an Audrey Hepburn movie called *Breakfast At Tiffany's*. Audrey's character dressed up and went to the jewelry store whenever she was depressed. We decided to give it a try. After that, Kiki and I put on disguises, dressed elegantly, and visited jewelry stores and dress shops. We tried on their merchandise even though we had no intention of buying anything."

"Shame on you," laughed Heather.

"Once, after we'd driven a jeweler nearly crazy trying on every watch in his shop, other customers came in and he began helping them, too. Kiki and I eventually left. Later that evening she realized she was still wearing one of his expensive watches."

"And . . . ," prompted the bed-ridden law enforcement officer.

"We weren't thieves," Myrtle scolded. "She took the watch back the next morning."

"Perfect," breathed a listener, laying earphones aside. "Installing those listening devices at the Samuelson's is giving us information we didn't expect. Now that they've connected the dots for us, we'll be able to get another one of our projects taken care of."

"Why not let the doc handle it?"

"That's a great idea. I'll put a few incentives together and mail it to him anonymously. We'll see how upset he really is."

###

WHAT IS KIKI'S SIDELINE?

To answer this question, follow directions for a four-word clue.

_ _ _ _   _ _ _   _ _ _ _ _   _ _ _ _ _ _ _ _

Start with letter X:
Move one space north.
Move two spaces north and two spaces west.
Move two spaces east.
Move one space west.
Move three spaces west and three spaces south.
Move three spaces north.
Move two spaces east and two spaces south.
Move one space east.
Move two spaces north and two spaces west
Move one space west and one space south.
Move four spaces east.
Move two spaces south and one space west.
Move one space west.
Move two spaces west and one space north
Move one space east.
Move one space east.
Move one space north.
Move one space south.
Move one space east and one space north.
Move two spaces west
Move two spaces south.

H	H	S	N	I
A	L	V	R	N
C	L	E	R	U
G	Y	S	D	X

CHAPTER 10

"It's good of you to see me," Heather said when she stopped at Worldwide Courier and Delivery Service the next morning.

"How can I help you?" the manager asked, raising a limp hand to be shaken.

"I'd like to know something about your company before I commit to anything," Heather said, settling at the edge of the chair opposite the manager. "I occasionally need things delivered, but I'm also interested in what it takes to become a courier."

"Are you applying for a job?" He settled stiffly in his padded chair.

"Not until I know more about the company. How long has Worldwide Courier been in business?"

"Thirty-five years." He pushed a brochure across his desk. "Here's a list of our various branches."

Heather studied the brochure and smiled. "There's one in Boston. I have friends who work for the company. I think they got their start in the Boston office. I don't suppose you know Kiki Kelly?"

The manager sighed. "I don't discuss our employees."

"A neighbor of mine, Inez Perkins, told me she works for you. She said she was headed for Taiwan this trip. She loves going to so many different places." Heather leaned forward. "How often does she get to travel out of the country over a year's time?"

"This year she's been to most of the fifty States, plus Hong Kong, Amsterdam, and Paris." He paused. "We save most of our overseas deliveries for her because, over the years, she's made so many contacts—airline personnel, cab drivers, shop owners; that sort of thing."

"Do you require more education than just a high school diploma?"

"We've gotten choosey. Rather than a collection of degrees, we prefer employees with experience in law enforcement or security work. Our people have to pass rigid physical standards, weapons qualification tests, and first aid training."

"Are you saying that your couriers carry weapons?"

"Sometimes they do, yes."

"I don't remember Inez mentioning a background in security or law enforcement." When the manager didn't respond, Heather added, "Have any of your employees ever been charged with a crime?"

The puffy eyes of the manager opened wide. "We always check backgrounds. If there was anything like that in someone's background, they wouldn't be working for us." He looked at Heather more closely. "Exactly what do you have in mind?"

"Like Inez I'm a single woman who itches to see more of the world. You'd be disappointed in me as an employee if I didn't do the same kind of thorough background checking on prospective employers as they will do on me. Don't other people ask you questions like this?"

The manager studied Heather, then said, "Is there anything else you need to know?"

"You've been very helpful," Heather said, getting to her feet. "I'll get back to you once I've made a decision."

As she walked out the door she overheard the manager ask his secretary to send a note to Inez to tell her one more person had been asking about her. Slowly the door closed, but not before Heather heard the manager add, "This lady didn't leave her name either, and she asked the same questions as that short guy with the missing finger."

As Heather walked past the building once owned by her father, a shiver raced up her back. Abruptly she turned in. Stopping here might answer questions, but it would also bring back painful memories.

"May I help you?" The receptionist's name plate identified her as Marta. She was new to the office since Heather's last visit.

"I'd like to see Daniel Baxter, please."

"Do you have an appointment?" Marta looked first at her appointment book and then at Heather.

"Please tell him Heather Samuelson would like a few minutes of his time."

The receptionist frowned, but called Daniel Baxter, president of what had once been Samuelson and Baxter, CPA Group.

"Heather," greeted the portly man who had been Charlie Samuelson's partner and best friend. "How good of you to stop. Come in and let's get caught up." He escorted Heather to his private office where she sat in a chair opposite the desk once occupied by her father.

"Dan, I won't stay long. I know you're busy."

"I'm never too busy for one of Charlie's girls. We haven't seen any of you since your mother's memorial service." He leaned back in his chair, concentrating on the troubled face opposite him.

"We're all busy, either with our careers or raising kids." She paused. "I need answers to some questions, and I didn't know where else to go for information."

Dan nodded agreeably. "Ask away."

"I know you and Dad were experienced fraud examiners, called as expert witnesses whenever the courts needed someone to tie down a case."

Dan nodded. "The firm still gets those assignments since we have a good reputation in that field."

"Tell me what happened eight years ago when all of the Samuelson girls were out of town."

"Are you asking about a particular case?" Dan looked puzzled.

"Joel Bishop's. How did the firm figure into that?"

Dan Baxter clasped his hands together and took a deep breath. "I'll answer your questions, but I'd like your assurance the answers won't become common knowledge. I don't want Joel Bishop to remember this firm even exists."

Heather ran her fingers across her lips in a zipping motion, and Dan smiled at the youthful gesture. He leaned back in his chair once more.

"Back then, Charlie and I specialized in forensic and investigative checks where misappropriation of funds or fraud was suspected. We often performed audits without the knowledge of the alleged embezzler. In Bishop's case, Charlie discovered that all the custodial authorization and record keeping functions of the company resided in one individual."

"Bishop himself?"

"Right. At that time his company had government contracts, and with everything in his hands, he could put his new wife and her three youngsters on the payroll without it sounding an alarm. He diverted roughly a million dollars a month into their combined salaries, all of which ended up in a bank account with his name on it. He had a bookkeeping system so complicated that when annual audits took place no one found the problems because they were buried so deep. Charlie, of course, figured it out and the matter went to trial."

Heather nodded. So far Dan Baxter's account agreed with her speculations as she unraveled her mother's puzzle letter.

"There was a federal indictment because of the government contracts, so Bishop's case went to federal court."

"And Dad?"

"Because Charlie uncovered the looting, he was the government's expert witness."

"How did the murders figure into the trial?" Heather referred to Joel Bishop's murder of his former wife and her children.

"Elayne was set to testify, along with her sister Brenda." Dan Baxter picked up his pencil and drummed it nervously.

"And the children?"

More nervous drumming. "They were Elayne's by a previous marriage and ranged in age from two to twelve. As for the kids, there wasn't anything they could add to the trial that wasn't being said by others."

"So the children really didn't figure in?"

"Only so far as Bishop trying to influence Elayne's testimony by threatening their lives. It didn't work. She wouldn't back down." Dan paused before going on. "The night before she was to testify, she and the kids had a car accident. Only it wasn't an accident. They all died, and that brought more witnesses into the proceedings. Of course Charlie started it all by notifying the feds of the looting. Everything eventually came crashing down on Bishop. As a result he was convicted of fraud, and later of four counts of murder."

"According to stories I've read, he threatened everyone and anyone who had a hand in putting him behind bars. Do you think he was able to follow through on his threats?"

"Joel Bishop is not a nice man, Heather. I'm sure he has enough money hidden in various locations that he can get done, whatever it is he wants done, except, I hope, buying his way out of prison."

"Is he still appealing his convictions?"

"I haven't checked recently, but I doubt he's exhausted the system yet."

"If he won his appeal, would there be a retrial?"

"Undoubtedly. It would mean there was an error in the first trial."

"Would all the former witnesses have to testify again?"

"Yes. At least those who are still alive."

Heather reached in her purse, and withdrew a newspaper clipping. "I have a picture I'd like you to look at. The caption doesn't identify everyone." She handed Dan Baxter the picture. Standing next to the man identified as Joel Bishop was a woman Heather knew as Eleanor Anderson.

Eleanor came into Heather's life in February after Mattie Samuelson's death. Eleanor said she knew Charlie because they were both part of a group trying to see that justice was done. When she asked about Charlie and learned of his death on Mt. Hood, she became extremely upset. She had invited Heather to join her later in the week, but when Heather returned two days later, Eleanor's house was empty.

Heather's search of moving companies failed to uncover the one responsible for relocating the Anderson family. Even the post office was unable to supply information. The woman simply vanished.

Dan was still studying the faded picture. "Of course the cocky looking one is Bishop," he said. "His legal eagles are on either side of him, and behind them are Elayne and Brenda."

Heather pointed to Eleanor Anderson. "That's Brenda? The sister-in-law?"

Daniel nodded.

"You asked me to promise this conversation wouldn't become common knowledge. Is that because you think Bishop might try something?"

Dan looked up, and handed the picture back to Heather. "I wasn't involved in the trial, so that should exclude me from any hit list he's prepared. However, he might take his anger at Charlie out on the firm."

"In what way? Do you think he'd set fire to the building?" Heather's stomach tightened.

Dan Baxter nodded. "I've tried to prepare for that eventuality. Electronic records are now kept in several off-site locations. There's not a lot I can do about protecting myself, except to drive carefully and look behind me fairly often."

"Why didn't Mom or Dad ever mention the trial to Rachel or Sally or me?"

"I'm sure they didn't want to worry you. There wasn't anything you could do. It was a time when all of us were busy watching our backs."

"I'd guess you're still doing some of that."

Dan Baxter nodded. "You'd be guessing correctly."

THE TIME HAS COME

L + 1 = M	D - 3 =	K + 1 =
E - 4 =		F + 3 =
N - 3 =		V - 3 =
C + 2 =		P + 4 =

M _ _ _   _   _ _ _ _

A + 2 =	G + 2 =	S + 1 =
F + 2 =	W - 3 =	T + 3 =
A + 4 =		L - 3 =
G - 4 =		H - 5 =
I + 2 =		B + 3 =

_ _ _ _ _   _ _   _ _ _ _ _

CHAPTER 11

When Heather returned from visiting her father's former business partner, she opened her mother's scrapbook and looked once more at the death notices and obituaries. She pulled out the oldest, then grabbed a notebook and pen, and began making a list.

Webbler, Maxine. Age 42. Date of death: April 19, 2000.

Heather flipped phone book pages, looking for the name *Webbler.* Two were listed in town. She dialed Mina Webbler and waited. On the third ring a woman answered, talking loudly over the sounds of children arguing in the background. "Hello?"

"Is this Mina Webbler?"

"Yes. Could you speak up?"

Heather raised her voice, "My name is Heather Samuelson and I live in Lewisburg. I'm calling about Maxine Webbler. Did you know her?" Heather's stomach contracted as she waited for an answer.

She heard a gasp. "Maxine? What about her?"

"My mom, who is now deceased, kept a copy of Maxine's obituary. I've been wondering if Mom and Maxine were friends. My mom was Mattie Samuelson."

"I wouldn't know anything about my mother-in-law's friends."

"Do you know if Maxine ever served on a jury?"

A silence followed, then the line clicked, dead.

Heather looked at the buzzing receiver. "So much for that lead. If I had to guess, I'd say I touched a sensitive spot and Maxine may have been involved in Joel Bishop's trial." She picked up the obituary clippings again. "Who's next?"

Henry Cooper. Age 59. Date of death: September 3, 2000.

With the phone book at her side, Heather began dialing the Lewisburg Coopers.

"Hello?" A deep male voice boomed the greeting.

"Is this William Cooper?"

"Who wants to know?"

"I'm Heather Samuelson and I live in Lewisburg. I'm trying to close my mother's estate and make sense out of things she collected."

"So? Why are you calling me?"

"She saved a death notice for Henry Cooper. Did you know him?"

There was a pause before the man responded quietly, "He was my dad."

"As far as I know, my mom never met him so I don't know why she saved his obituary. Could you tell me how he died?"

"Hit and run. Some bastard went out of his way to cream Dad as he got mail from the letter box."

"Was your dad ever involved in a trial, maybe as a witness or a juror?"

"Who'd you say you was?"

"Heather Samuelson. I'm in the phone book and I live at the Taborhill Garden Estates."

"Dad had jury duty a couple of times. Why?"

"Was one of the trials regarding Joel Bishop?"

There was a pause. "I don't know why you're asking these questions, lady. Dad's death was hard on our family, and we don't want no one reminding us. They never did catch the bastard who nailed him."

"Couldn't you just tell me if he ever had anything to do with Joel Bishop's trial?"

After another pause the baritone voice whispered, "Yes. Now don't you never call us again."

Bingo, Heather congratulated herself, shuffling obituary and death notices.

Next death notice: *Ed Moore. Age 42. Date of death: January 22, 2001.*

Heather looked up the Moore families in Lewisburg and began dialing. Her fourth call was answered by Emily Moore. She not only knew Ed, but seemed eager to talk about him. He'd been a neighbor with the same last name; not a relative.

"I remember Ed," Emily said. "Nice man. He liked to grow sunflowers. Our neighborhood got real excited when he was called to jury duty on that important trial we had in the late '90's. We thought we'd get lots of unpublished details once it was over, because we had another neighbor on the same jury."

"What was that neighbor's name?" Heather asked.

"Bob Carlson."

Heather scanned the remaining obituaries. Nothing for Bob Carlson. "Does Mr. Carlson still live near you?"

"No. He moved. Left about the time Ed died. One day the Carlsons were neighbors and the next day they moved without telling anyone where they were going. It was real surprising since they'd lived here for twenty years."

"Do you remember how Ed died?"

"Sure do. Cops thought it was a burglary gone bad 'cause he was shot in his own house. In the bedroom, as I remember. Never did hear that they caught the killer."

Heather thanked Emily and added a few lines to her notes. It looked like Mattie had known the names of people involved in Joel Bishop's trial, and had been cataloging their deaths.

It also looked as if Joel Bishop found someone to carry out his death threat to those involved in his trial.

"Did you get Jake Lundeen's phone message," Myrtle asked as she passed Heather on her way to answer the doorbell.

Heather looked up from her notes and shook her head.

"He said, and I quote '*If'n you bring some pills, I'll tell you what that lady and Doc Adams talked about. But you better hurry. My memory ain't what it used to be.*'" Myrtle was laughing as she opened the door. "Jazz," she greeted, inviting him in.

"I thought I'd see if you ladies needed a break from nursing our invalid."

"Right on time," Myrtle replied. "Heather has to visit Mr. Lundeen at The Boardwalk and I want to go with her."

"That's why I'm here. Let's see if Sally needs anything before you leave."

###

After a stop at a grocery store, Heather and Myrtle greeted Jake at The Boardwalk.

"These are the best yet," he said, his voice low as he unwrapped a mint. "Good pills. They help me remember things real clear."

"You said you overheard what Doc and Kiki talked about," Heather prompted, her voice low. Then she noticed the second bed was unoccupied. "Where's Doc?"

"He's at physical therapy, getting a water treatment. That's why I wanted you here now."

"What did you hear Kiki say?" Myrtle asked.

"That lady told Doc she's famous." Jake popped the unwrapped mint in his mouth and chewed on it. Then he said, "Doc told her he'd been reading about her and was glad she still had good hands. He told her she was the only student who hadn't gone to jail." Jake unwrapped another mint. "Whatta you make'a that?" He popped the mint in his mouth, then added, "Should'a mentioned first off how she showed up dressed like a man. Thought she was 'til she started talking."

When Jake said that was all he'd heard, the women thanked him and left.

Myrtle said, "I wonder what Kiki did to become famous?" A big smile lit her face. "I get a charge out of hearing she's still using disguises."

"I hope Sally's able to check on her background. Kiki may have served jail time that Doc wasn't aware of. We shouldn't rule that out. Maybe your friend didn't stick to magic tricks."

Back home, Myrtle climbed the stairs to Sally's room to relieve Jazz, who headed back to work. Heather walked to the intersection next to the Perkins' house where an electrician from Aba Brothers Electrical was working on the street light.

"Can't you get that light to stay on?" she asked. Above the man's pocket was the name Leonardo. "What's the problem?"

"Someone's messing with it," the electrician said. "That's the problem. I told Mr. Keyes he'd better keep an eye out for whoever's disabling this baby. They might be planning more burglaries."

"Do your best," Heather said, moving on to the Keyes' townhouse. She rang the doorbell.

"Yes," answered Vera Keyes, leaning heavily on her walker. She was a frail-looking woman of about forty. Her weathered face was topped by a full head of vibrant red hair.

"Mrs. Keyes, we met recently. I'm Heather Samuelson. Is Brad home? I should talk to him about the street light that's being vandalized."

"I'm the one you want to talk to about that. Come on in."

Heather followed Vera into the house. "What are we going to do about keeping that light working? The electrician just told me someone's *messing* with it."

"I've been watching," Vera responded, her bottom lip quivering. "It's bad enough being crippled, and having robberies going on all around me, without having the street light out so's it's easier to steal things." Vera remembered her manners and added, "Have a seat."

Heather settled in a chair as Vera continued, "I've got myself set up to listen for things going on in that woman's house." She pointed toward the wall connecting the two townhouses. "I heard that burglar going through her things the other night, but thought it was that lady home again."

"Then you didn't hear anything that caused you to sound an alarm?"

"Nope. Just thought she'd come home. She comes and goes like some kind of ghost in the night. Most unfriendly woman I ever met. Never speaks or waves. Just drives in and out like some delivery person." At that moment, Vera's daughter entered the house.

"Hi, Miz Samuelson," Stormy said. She looked at her mother and laughed. "Has Ma been telling you about her new listening device?"

Heather looked from Stormy to Vera and back.

"Shame on you telling our little secrets," Vera scolded with a sly smile. "Why're you home instead of in class?"

"The professor didn't show up. We waited the mandatory ten minutes and then everyone got out of there as fast as they could." Stormy added, "Can I fix tea for anyone? Ma?"

"If you don't mind," Vera responded as her daughter left the room.

Heather looked at Vera. "What's this listening device Stormy mentioned?"

Vera sighed and reached out to upend the empty water glass beside her. She placed the base of it against the wall connecting her living room with Inez's. Satisfied, she put her ear at the open end.

"Are you telling me you're able to hear what goes on in Inez's house with that contraption?"

"Didn't they tell you the man who built these places went bankrupt? He must'a been cutting corners any way he could. With a glass like this I can almost hear breathing next door. I don't know how that builder got inspectors to pass on his work. Probably slipped them something on the side. I knew you were in that house yesterday afternoon when a phone call came in. How'd you manage that?"

"Doc's renter asked me to let the glazier in. She gave me a key."

"That'll come in handy if there's another robbery. Hang on to it."

TWO WORDS THAT RELATE TO THE KEYES FAMILY

List something they are short of and something they do too much of.

Add one letter to each of the words below, forming a new word. The addition may be at the beginning, end, or within the word. Place the added letter on the line below the boxes. The added letters, reading from left to right, will form a 4-letter and a 9-letter word.

A, A, C, D, E, E, H, O, P, R, S, S, V

heat	bed	talk	tree
cheat			

_____C_____

rob	lone	seen	dad	eat	one	fog	cat	late
robe								

_____E_____

CHAPTER 12

"Look what they brought me," Sally called from her bed when Heather returned from talking to Vera Keyes. Sally motioned toward a laptop. A list of subjects assigned to her was taped to it.

Heather smiled. "I'm glad you'll have something to keep you busy. Let me know when you have any information." Sally had promised to check on Eleanor and Travis Anderson, and Brenda Ethan, Eleanor's real name. Heather was eager to learn details.

Sally searched frantically among her blankets, finally producing a slip of paper she handed to Heather. "Read this when you have time," she said as the doorbell rang.

Heather hurried down the stairs, glancing at Sally's note as she went.

"We have bugs in the house," Sally had written. *"Watch what you say. We'll talk later."*

Heather sucked in a sharp breath. *Bugs? Did Sally mean listening devices?* The thought was numbing. Heather moved toward the front door like a sleepwalker. She opened it slowly. "Dr. Evans!" she greeted, her mind still sorting questions. *A listening device? In their new house? Why? Who put it there, and for how long had someone been eavesdropping?*

"Hi, Heather," Dr. Evans said. "I thought I'd see how my patient is doing. I get an occasional afternoon off and this happens to be it."

"Of course," she mumbled. "Come in." *Who would care what the Samuelson sisters said? Was the device left over from the previous owner—the thief who had hidden stolen gems in their attic?*

Dr. Evans followed Heather upstairs and into Sally's room. "I see you're following doctor's orders," he said, pulling out his stethoscope.

"Brought me a bedpan, I bet," Sally responded. "When can I get this cast-thing off?"

Dr. Evans laughed. "The bedpan comes on the next trip, along with the crutches. Have you been putting ice packs on your leg three or four times a day?"

"Yes," Sally answered, uncovering her leg.

"How about pain pills? Are you still taking them?"

"I haven't had any today."

"Good for you. I assume you have help going to the bathroom?" He smiled at Myrtle and Heather, both nodding their heads. "In another few days, we'll see about fitting you with something that lends itself to moving more easily on your own." Dr. Evans pulled blankets back over Sally's leg, looked at his watch, then said, "See you in a day or two." He let Heather show him out of the house.

"You didn't say whether Sally's leg is healing as it should," Heather prompted.

"It looks fine. That's why I'll bring crutches in a day or two. That'll be soon enough for her to put weight on her leg. Keep elevating it, but you can discontinue the ice." He opened his car door. "I suppose the lady who caused the accident is off on another trip."

Heather nodded.

"Which house is hers?" He waited while Heather pointed. "She certainly lives close, doesn't she? I'm sorry she's gone. I'm planning to make an offer for her ring—one she can't refuse."

"You got a call from Coffman Jewelers while you were outside with Dr. Evans," Sally reported when Heather returned. She was playing another game of cribbage with Myrtle. "Abe wants to meet with you in person as soon as possible. He said to remind you that they close in two hours."

"But I want to talk to you," Heather whispered, taking Sally's note from her pocket and waving it.

"That'll keep," smiled Sally. "Take care of your client while I trounce Aunt Myrtle."

It was against Heather's better judgment to leave without discussing the listening devices, but nothing fired her imagination like the idea that a customer might not be content with her work. When she finished with her client, she wanted details concerning listening devices in their home. They needed to figure out who was interested in their conversations, and why.

###

When Heather entered Coffman Jewelers she found Abe working on a design of some kind. He quickly stood to his full height, somewhere close to five feet, and rushed to greet her. His dark eyes snapped with excitement.

"You came. Thank you. I was worried you were so busy with your sister you might not be able to work me into your schedule today. Is she going to be all right?" He buttoned his suit coat as he spoke.

Abe had taken over the business when his father died. As a second generation Coffman engaged in designing and selling jewelry, he had nearly been forced to close shop when a robbery forced him into bankruptcy. Thankfully, a friend offered him a way to stay in business. Abe accepted the friend's offer. It was something he never talked about except to say how thankful he was to have such a good friend.

"Sally will be fine." Heather smiled at his concern. "What can I do for you?" She waited for him to supply the reason he'd requested a meeting.

"I'm worried." He reached under his counter and pulled out a paper. "I want to make sure there's nothing about my new website that encourages crooks to steal my merchandise. Every time I read about phishing and spoofing I feel ill." He handed the printed page to Heather.

'Where did you get this?" she asked.

"Off the internet."

Heather skimmed the story of a distraction robbery that had taken place that morning in Taipei. The robber told the jeweler he wanted to look at several pieces being advertised. Without exception, they were the most expensive jewels in the shop. The jeweler was careful to show one piece at a time, but as questions were asked about the color, cut, clarity and carats, more and more of the expensive pieces were soon lined up on the countertop. That was the last thing the jeweler clearly remembered. After a while he realized a significant number of his jewels, and his customer, were gone.

"Mr. Coffman," Heather handed the article back. "This crime didn't take place online. This jeweler should have had several cameras operating, and a policy of showing only one piece of jewelry at a time."

"That was the policy," Abe replied, "but apparently he got too excited about making a big sale."

"Having another clerk on duty would have helped." Heather looked around Abe's shop, noticing several video cameras. "Do all those work?"

"Yes."

"Then as long as you show only one piece of jewelry at a time, and get money from credit card purchases before mailing any merchandise, you'll be in good shape."

"I better be. Coffman Jewelers couldn't stand another big loss."

"You've had robberies in the past?"

"Two. The first was in 1971 when Dad was new to the business. He went to an international jewelers' convention. A theft took place that nearly ended Coffman Jewelers. His partner at that time was wiped out and committed suicide. I was a teenager then. Our second robbery took place in 1998. It, too, almost wiped out Coffman Jewelers. I was lucky to be offered a business contract that has allowed me to recover financially and stay in business."

"Your business has now entered the new millennium with up-to-date security in place." Heather waved her hand to include the cameras focused on her.

"Thanks for reassuring me, Heather. I got a call recently about a designer ring that was stolen in the 1998 heist. Apparently it, or a copy, has turned up. We jewelers work hard to create pieces that are original. If there's more than one copy running around, then someone has gone to a lot of trouble to duplicate our work, or it isn't a copy, and it's our original piece that's turned up."

"I can't imagine there being enough designs in the world to *not* become repetitious," Heather said.

"Most designers try to turn out styles that any knowledgeable jeweler can recognize." He reached into the case beside him and withdrew a ring. "Notice the design in the filigree beside the stones." He passed her a magnifying glass and the expensive ring, then selected a pair of earrings. He handed her the earrings. "You'll see the same design nestled around the stones in the earrings."

Heather nodded, noticing once more Abe's short index finger as he pointed at the patterns. The finger lacked the first two joints. She'd overheard the manager of Worldwide Courier tell his secretary about a "short guy with a missing finger." Could that have been Abe?

"Dad was the first jeweler to come up with the idea of designs," Abe bragged. "Now, anyone in the business can look at an expensive piece and figure out where it came from."

"Does every jeweler do something like this?"

Abe nodded. "We specialize in various designs and combinations of designs such as abstract and modern, art nouveau or Celtic. Some enclose animal or plant forms."

Heather handed the jewelry back to Abe. "Thanks for the lesson, Mr. Coffman. I'm going home to finish your website. It should be up and running by evening."

"Wait a minute. I want you to see the highlight of my offerings. I'm finally putting my most expensive piece up for sale."

"You mean the Duchess Diamonds?" Heather asked. "I remember when the *Clarion* did a feature on them."

Abe smiled and turned to the wall safe behind him. He spun the dial several times before removing an expensive looking box. "I took these out of storage." He handed the box to Heather. "Open it, but please don't touch the stones."

Heather opened the box and discovered she'd forgotten how to breathe. The grouping of brilliant stones known as the Duchess Diamonds, each over two karats, was unlike anything she'd seen before. The twist of large stones formed a magnificent drop pendant set in white gold. It had been designed for a long-forgotten Duchess in the eighteenth century.

"I'd like you to include a picture of these on my website."

"You're really selling them?"

"They're jinxed. It's time someone else got the benefit of what they draw to them." Smiling sadly Abe closed the elegant box and returned it to his safe, then handed Heather a digital camera containing a picture of the diamonds. "Use this to get a good picture for the website. When will it be up and running?"

"In about an hour," Heather responded.

Abe said, "I've been meaning to ask if I've taken you away from your visitors? That's a nice new van they're driving."

Heather looked startled. "That's my van."

"Really? I drive past Taborhill Estates every day on my way to and from work. I thought the van meant you had company."

"We do have company, but the van is mine." Heather glanced at the time. "Nice talking to you, Mr. Coffman. I'm headed home to get your website operational. Let me know if you have any other concerns."

After an hour of quiet concentration, Heather finished the Coffman website. She put it in service just as there was a quiet knock at the front door. She pushed away from her computer and hurried down the stairs. Standing at her front door was Father Raymond Adams. He was carrying a large box.

"Hello," she greeted. "Won't you come in?"

He followed her into the living room and sat down. The box rested on his lap. "I'm only staying a few minutes so I'll decline any offers of coffee or tea," he said, anticipating Heather's invitation.

She nodded, sitting down across from him.

Father Adams studied the young woman. "I'm here because you've asked questions about Dad and his renter. I got to thinking, after your last visit, that there were a couple boxes I hadn't sorted yet. I started checking the contents yesterday and found this one contains things that will probably never mean anything to anyone except Dad." Father Adams reached into the box and lifted out a jumble of clippings.

"Those look old," Heather commented.

"They are. Dad's written dates on many of them, some of which date back to the seventies."

"His collection reminds me of things I found after my mother's death. I'm still trying to discover their significance."

Father Adams smiled. "I was getting ready to throw these away, but then I saw the name of that woman you were asking about. I decided there might be something in here that would answer your questions.

Since Dad's been at The Boardwalk, he doesn't clip things any more, but he occasionally asks me to put a page from the newspaper with the collection."

"Don't you think he'll want you to hold on to these?"

Father Adams shook his head. "Dad had a setback last night after his hydrotherapy. His health seems to be going downhill these past few weeks. However, if you find anything in here that refers to him that I should know about, save it for me. I would also appreciate knowing the next time his renter is in town."

Heather nodded and accepted the box. After escorting her visitor to the door, she took the box upstairs to Sally's room. Luckily the cribbage tournament had ended and Myrtle had gone to the kitchen to fix dinner. However, a voice recorder was playing, and it sounded like the cribbage game was still in progress. Sally motioned toward the recorder, then held her fist beside an ear as if listening to a receiver. Heather nodded her understanding

"Father Adams brought this," Heather whispered. She held it so Sally could observe the confusion of newspaper clippings.

"Another person saving newspaper articles?" Sally kept her voice low.

Heather nodded.

Sally whispered, "Put it at the foot of my bed, then take this." She handed Heather a tablet and a pen. At the top of the tablet was written: *We'd better communicate like this, in case our computers have been compromised.*

Heather nodded and wrote: *what gives?* She waited quietly for an answer.

Sally responded: *My buddies thought it was a joke when they brought their new bug tracking device along with the laptop, but they found we're infested. Too many and too new to be leftovers from the Tom Fuely days.*

"*Where?*"

"*Living room, dining room, three bedrooms.*"

"*Why? Who? Let's get rid of them.*"

Sally wrote: *Let's wait. We don't talk about cop things. All we've discussed recently is Inez. Can't think of anything else that has a mystery attached.*

"Oh God," Heather whispered. She wrote: *Mom's letter.*

Sally nodded, watching as Heather scribbled rapidly: *Whoever is listening may work for Joel Bishop. He may also know I'm headed to Dover on the fifteenth, hoping to make contact with Dad.*

###

WHO CARES?

There's a killer in the wings, a burglar in the foreground, and a main character using an alias. Which one of these individuals cares what two sisters and their aunt talk about?

BURN, COULD, DEVIL, FRIEND, MORE, ERODE, THREE, EVERY

Match the words above with the words below. Then remove a letter from the beginning, middle or end of each of the words above to create a new word. When the letter removed is put in the column to the right, in the correct order, you will find the answer to the above question.

Hints	New Word	Letter removed
ADDITIONAL	more	M
WAS ABLE	could	U
BLIND MICE	_____	—
FIX EGGS	_____	—
WASH AWAY	_____	—
PAL	_____	—
ALL	_____	—
COOK TOO LONG	_____	—

CHAPTER 13

After a restless night, Heather phoned Jazz. "If your invitation to go for coffee this morning is still open, I'm available."

Jazz paused, then laughed, "Are you? Well, why don't I pick you up in a few minutes?"

Heather agreed, hung up the phone, and stopped at Sally's bedroom door. "I'm going to coffee with Jazz. Could I bring either of you anything?" Sally and Myrtle were sorting Doc Adam's clippings.

Sally said, "Thanks, but I'm probably going to spend the day playing a few card games. Then I'll take a nap."

"After I beat your sister a few more times, I'm going to return to my knitting." Myrtle added, "You know, knit one, purl two." She smiled and continued sorting clippings. "But I would very much like a white chocolate . . . ."

"Again?" laughed Heather as the doorbell sounded. "I've got your special order memorized, Auntie. See you two later."

"What's going on?" Jazz asked as he and Heather walked from the house. "We both know I didn't suggest coffee this morning." He noted her van parked in a neighbor's carport.

"Could we take my car," Heather asked, "and you drive?"

"We can do that," he responded. They walked to Inez's carport to retrieve the van. "Any place special you want to go?"

"Just drive for a while, please."

Jazz drove to the hills west of town, then parked. "Okay, what gives? What's upset you?" Heather had been systematically shredding a tissue.

She blinked back tears and looked up. "Sally's buddies brought her a laptop so she could continue working on her caseload. They thought they were being funny when they brought along a new bug detector to show off, but after they found five in our house, everyone stopped laughing."

"Why would anyone want to bug your place?"

"I'd like to tell you what I think it's about, but I can't. What scares me is that I may have put someone's life at risk."

Jazz studied Heather's worried expression then reached for her hands. "Are you thinking the listening devices have something to do with your mom's scrapbook?"

Shock registered on Heather's face.

"What do you know about Mom's scrapbook?"

"Probably everything. What exactly have you figured out?" He released her hands and gently brushed a wisp of hair from her face.

"I think the threat Joel Bishop made at his trial is real. I think he's hired an assassin who's making good on that threat."

"You may be right. But don't sell law enforcement short. They'll be working hard to head off any murders, even if they won't talk about it. If it reassures you, there's an unofficial task force of two working on it independently."

Heather stared at him. "You and who else?"

"Sergeant Miller. Ox and I have been friends forever and I trust him." He paused. "Because you are operating your design company from home, it's rare that both you and Sally are out of the house at the same time. I suspect the *Clarion*'s story of her accident alerted someone to a window of opportunity to install those devices. Sally was in the hospital and you went to visit her. The day you found wet footprints on your carpeting was probably when the devices were installed." He studied her face. "Do you think the bugs are connected with someone trying to make sure your dad is really dead?"

As Heather's eyes filled with tears, she blinked several times. "That's what I'm afraid of. I talked to my sisters about my suspicions, before we knew about the eavesdropping. I told them where I thought Dad will be and when he'd be there. If that's why the devices were installed, then I may have set him up as a target for Bishop's assassin."

###

Sally whispered in Myrtle's ear, "Let's put the clippings in order, oldest first."

Myrtle nodded and began rearranging the clippings. Just as they finished sorting, they heard Heather climbing the stairs.

"How's everyone feeling?" She handed Myrtle her white chocolate mocha. "Are you better?" She pantomimed a receiver at her ear and mouthed, "Where?"

Sally pointed at the valance at the top of her window. Heather moved closer, finally spotting a small device behind the valance. She nodded and created a cloth cradle for her iPod. "You'll feel better with a little soft music to lull you to sleep," she said, pinning the cradle on the valance, opposite the listening device. When she turned the iPod on, music filled the air.

Sally handed Heather the clippings she and Myrtle had assembled. The oldest one, dated 1962, told of a series of jewel robberies in Idaho. The culprit's capture was expected momentarily. In pencil at the top of the article was written *H.A.* The next clipping, dated 1968, was an ad for a magic school in Idaho, promising former full-time professionals as instructors.

Next was a clipping from 1971, detailing the theft of more than a million dollars' worth of jewels stolen by a trio at an international jeweler's convention in Detroit. A witness reported seeing sales staff cowering under display cases while robbers smashed cases and grabbed jewels. The thieves were dressed alike, each with a dust mask to protect against inhaling glass dust. They fled the scene within two minutes. Given the confusion of breaking glass and the threat of bodily harm, patrons and sellers alike had panicked. Those not cowering rushed to escape. In the process a young man carrying a small boy was knocked to the floor. A showcase nearby shattered and knife-like shards struck the pair. The man died of his injuries at the scene, and the boy was in critical condition.

Penciled at the top of that article was *Tom, Dick and Harvey.*

A clipping from three days later identified the deceased shopper as Robert Perkins. His son Kevin, age four, was listed in critical condition.

The three Samuelson women stared at one another, silently mouthing, "Perkins? Inez?"

Heather picked up the next clipping. It too told of a jewel robbery. Penciled in the margin were the letters *SJ*.

Next, dated a year later, was a story from an Idaho newspaper advertising the unforgettable, spellbinding skills of Magic Kiki. It promised floating objects, vanishing phenomenon, and thrilling surprises. The accompanying picture showed a young woman in a black cape, cards floating in the air around her.

"If Doc and Inez were both magicians," Heather whispered, "that could be their connection prior to the 1973 house Inez bought and put in Doc's name."

Sally nodded. "For some reason, Doc was saving clippings before they met."

"See if you can find a marriage license for Kathleen Kelly and Robert Perkins," Heather said.

Sally nodded and reached for her computer. In a low voice she said, "If I can't find that information with this machine, I'll phone someone at the office who has access to more sophisticated locater programs."

"I have two other items I'd like you to check on."

"Okay."

"Worldwide Courier told me they prefer hiring people with law enforcement or security backgrounds. See if that describes Inez."

"And?"

"The old man who shares a room with Doc said Inez visited Doc yesterday. Jake heard Doc tell her that she was his only student who hadn't been in jail. Could you check on that?"

Sally nodded. "If Doc's students ended up in jail, it's possible he spent time there, too. What's his full name?"

"Harold Adams."

Sally began researching.

"Did you get the Samuelson girl calmed down?" Ox asked when Jazz returned to the office.

"Pretty much. I think Bishop's hit man is tracking the sisters. Five listening devices are in the girls' house."

"Five? Those girls will be holding all their meetings in the bathroom. Are they going to junk the devices?"

Jazz shook his head. "I suspect they'll use them to give out bad information."

"That'll keep things stirred up, especially if the eavesdroppers believe what they hear."

As Heather researched more of the names from the obituaries her mother had collected, it occurred to her that if Bishop's hit man pushed her mother down a flight of stairs eight or nine years earlier, he might also have arranged for Mattie's murder to look like an accident. Perhaps it was time to make sure her death in February really was an accident.

"Back in an hour," Heather whispered, waving to Myrtle and Sally as she headed down the stairs. With a copy of her mother's accident report in hand, Heather stopped at a flower shop, then headed for the home of Benjamin Potter. It was time she got a look at the man whose vehicle was responsible for sending her mother's car into the flood waters of the Lewis River.

The Potter farmhouse on the outskirts of Lewisburg was in disrepair. Obviously the family could use extra cash. Had that need made them willing recipients of a Joel Bishop offer of some kind? Heather paused to take in the freshly cut lawn and poor condition of the buildings. Then, with the bouquet of flowers she'd purchased, she went to the door and knocked.

"Yes?" The woman standing in the doorway brushed grass clippings from her shoes. She had thin, shoulder-length gray hair and a fragile looking body.

"Mrs. Potter?" Heather glanced beyond her to an old man wrapped in an afghan, rocking slowly back and forth in a wooden rocker.

"Yes, I'm Amelia Potter."

"I'm Heather Samuelson."

The woman blanched, and looked quickly behind her. She stepped from the house and closed the door.

"You're one of Matilda Samuelson's daughters?"

"I am. I wondered if I could meet your husband. I'd like to tell him how much the message he sent through his minister, meant to my sisters and me." Heather was referring to the "please forgive me" message Benjamin Potter's minister forwarded after Benjamin's truck pushed Mattie's car into the flooded Lewis River.

"You don't understand," whispered Amelia. "Bennie hasn't been the same since that day. He feels so guilty for causing your mother's death. When her car went off the road into that water, they had to hold him back to keep him from trying to save her. He doesn't even know how to swim." A sob escaped. "He had to watch helplessly as she drowned." Amelia cleared her throat and with a grass-stained hand, wiped at a tear. "He just sits in that rocker, day after day, staring into space. He doesn't even drive anymore."

"I'm so sorry," Heather said. "I really wanted to meet him. I brought these flowers. Maybe . . . ." She paused, studying Mrs. Potter's face.

Amelia smiled for the first time. "Bennie loves flowers." She opened the door, gesturing for Heather to enter the house.

"Mr. Potter?" Heather walked slowly toward the man in the rocking chair. She held the flowers so he could see and smell them. "I heard you liked flowers, so I brought you some."

"F-flowers," he said, reaching for them. For a brief moment his eyes focused. Then he tipped his head back and sighed.

It was midnight when Heather's phone startled her awake. "Hello?"

"Heather," hissed the voice of Vera Keyes. "I can hear noises in that lady's house next door. Sounds like drawers opening and closing. Brad says there aren't any lights on and the only car in her carport is yours."

"Vera," Heather whispered. "Call 9-1-1, not me."

"And risk being called a crazy old woman? Or worse, a nosey one? I need to know first if I'm hearing things right. Get on over there and take that house key with you."

Heather crawled from bed and quietly moved into her office where Myrtle lay sleeping. She opened a desk drawer. From the Kiki Kelly file she removed Inez's house key, then crept down the stairs to slip on shoes and her raincoat. Taking her cell phone, a flashlight with a new battery, and Inez's house key, she made her way to the unoccupied house. Once again the troublesome street light was dark.

As Heather ducked under Inez's dining room windows, a soft thud inside the house startled her. Someone was in there all right. She pulled out her cell phone and punched in nine-one-one.

After reporting the problem, she quietly made her way to the back of the house where a garbage can leaned against the stairs into the house. Heather moved the can closer to the door, then returned to the side of the house and hunched down. She could see both the unlit street light in front of the Perkins' house, and the back door.

Unexpectedly, a voice rang out. "Heather, are you out here yet?" It sounded like Vera Keyes.

Heather remained quiet, not responding to the question.

At that moment a police car without flashers or a siren pulled up. Seconds later, a man bolted from the back door, and stumbled over the garbage can. "Back here," Heather yelled, as the thief pulled himself up and ran through Inez's backyard. One of the officers rushed to the back of the house and took off in the direction Heather pointed out. She hurried toward the front of the house to talk to the second policeman, surprised to see that the street light was no longer dark.

###

"I'm sorry to bother you, Inez." Heather had gone to the Kiki Kelly file and selected a phone number that reached her neighbor in whatever country she was visiting. "Your house was broken into a few hours ago. The thief got away with a few things, although he dropped some when he fell over the garbage can I put in his path."

"Why am I being singled out?"

"According to the police, almost ten percent of household burglaries are repeated within twelve months. Burglars return to collect goods left behind or goods they assume have been replaced."

"I'm guessing my alarm system didn't work."

"It didn't."

"What alerted the police?"

"Your neighbor. Vera Keyes heard activity inside your house. She called me and I hurried over. After I verified noises inside, I called the police."

"I suppose they didn't catch the fellow this time either."

"No, but he took away a few bruises."

"Thanks, Heather. I'm assuming the repairs to the hutch were made?"

"They were. I stayed until it was finished. You got a strange phone call while the hutch was being worked on."

"Yes, I know. I've listened to it. I'll be home in a day or two and I'll have the alarm system looked into again. Thanks for keeping me informed. I'm sorry it's turning out to be a bigger job than I anticipated."

"Father Adams asked to be notified the next time you're in town. His dad is losing ground and probably won't be with us much longer."

"Thanks. I appreciate knowing that."

###

"Found it," Sally whispered, pointing to the police department's laptop on the table beside her bed. A report was on the screen.

The iPod had been replaced with a recording of the afternoon cribbage game Myrtle and Sally played the day before. According to the recording, Myrtle was busy shuffling cards and Sally was complaining about her low score.

"What did you find?" Heather asked, trying unsuccessfully to read the laptop's details.

"It's a marriage license application for Kathleen Kelly and Robert Perkins, dated 1966 in the State of Massachusetts Vital Records."

"Way to go, Sally. Can you check death notices for Robert and Kevin Perkins?"

"Sure. After I finish a few department tasks."

"1966," Myrtle repeated. "Inez was two years ahead of me in high school and I graduated in 1967. That means she got married the year after she graduated. I wonder where she met Robert Perkins and what he did for a living."

Heather began making another list. "Kathleen Kelly graduated in 1965 and married the next year. We know that in 1971 she had a four-year-old son injured during a robbery. We found a 1972 clipping concerning Magic Kiki and we know she bought the house in Lewisburg in 1973."

"She told Doc Adams she's famous," Myrtle said. "And Doc is comfortable referring to her both as Inez and as Kiki."

"What's your point, Aunt Myrtle?"

"My point is; I wonder when she changed her name from Kathleen to Inez."

"It looks like that might have taken place soon after her husband's death."

"Poor Kiki," Myrtle said, heading for her bedroom. With Sally checking death notices for Robert and Kevin Perkins, it wouldn't be long before Heather returned to her computer. That meant the room Myrtle shared with the computer would no longer be private.

If Kiki was due home in a day or two, that should give Myrtle all the time she needed for what she had in mind. She hadn't been fully asleep the night before when Heather entered the room and removed a key from a folder that still lay on top of her desk. Myrtle eased her friend's house key from the folder, and returned to Sally's doorway. "I think I'll take a walk," she said. "I need some fresh air."

The sisters waved, paying little attention to their aunt.

Myrtle smiled and headed down the stairs. Heather had said the alarm system at Kiki's wasn't working, and that suited Myrtle just fine.

###

WHERE HAS MYRTLE GONE?

To answer this question, follow directions for a three-word clue.

— — — — — — — —   — — —   — — — — — — —

Start with letter X:
Move one space north.
Move two spaces north and two spaces west.
Move two spaces east.
Move one space west.
Move three spaces west and three spaces south.
Move three spaces north.
Move two spaces east and two spaces south.
Move one space east.
Move two spaces north and two spaces west
Move one space west and one space south.
Move four spaces east.
Move two spaces south and one space west.
Move one space west.
Move two spaces west and one space north
Move one space east.
Move one space north.
Move one space east.
Move one space east.
Move two spaces west and two spaces south.

H	G	E	R	A
F	W	E	R	O
N	S	I	N	S
C	S	A	R	X

CHAPTER 14

The stolen key opened both the front and the back doors of the Perkins'
house, making Myrtle's entry through the back door less obvious.
Remembering the alert neighbor on the other side of Kiki's wall,
Myrtle left the back door unlocked and tiptoed through the kitchen. It
was in her bedroom where she kept important papers. She hoped that's
where Kiki had hers. Quietly Myrtle climbed the stairs to the second
floor bedrooms.

In the first bedroom she searched dresser drawers, then the closet
and nightstand. After looking under the bed and checking under the
mattress, she moved to the second bedroom. Did all floors respond to
quiet footsteps as if Dumbo the elephant strolled across them? Myrtle
moved slowly, and as quietly as possible.

In the closet of the second bedroom she found boxes of papers that
turned out to be old tax forms. The forms were all for Kathleen Inez
Perkins. Myrtle flipped through the collection until she found forms for
1972 and 1973. She tucked them in the plastic bag she'd brought along.
They would be going home with her.

She reassembled the papers and returned the box to the closet. It
was then that she heard a door slam and footsteps running up the stairs.
Myrtle moved quickly into the closet beside the stacked boxes and
pulled the door shut. She was breathing heavily. The necklace she wore
danced on her chest as her heart pounded.

"I don't know where you are, Myrtle Wilson, but you can stop hiding
and get out here right this minute." The voice was Heather's. "I'm not
leaving until you show yourself so don't think you can outwait me."

Myrtle didn't move. She was reasonably sure she *could* outlast
Heather.

"You're going to have to pee pretty soon, and unless you want to
have an accident . . . ."

"Enough," called Myrtle, giving up before disaster struck. She opened the closet and stepped into the bedroom.

Heather moved from the hall into the bedroom. "Give me that key," she said, extending her hand.

Myrtle hung her head and handed the key to her niece, keeping the plastic bag with tax forms out of sight.

"Now get out of here so I can lock up. Inez phoned. She's due any minute and I've got to get my van out of her carport."

###

Back at the Samuelson house, Heather replaced the key, but took Kiki's file to her bedroom. She frowned at her aunt and pointed first at her; then at the guest room.

Myrtle knew when she was being sent to her room. She entered, closing the door behind her. There were papers she wanted to study, and she didn't want to be interrupted. She spread the stolen tax forms on her bed and searched through the 1972 copy, wishing she'd taken the form for 1971. That might have told her what Robert Perkins' occupation had been.

She scanned the documents until she found that Kiki's 1972 wages were paid by the State of Idaho, Corrections Division. In addition, one dependent was being claimed with deductible medical expenses attributed to Doernbecher Children's Hospital in Portland, Oregon.

Myrtle smiled. She was one step closer to learning what happened to her friend.

###

"Just thought I'd stop on my way to work," Dr. Evans explained as he checked Sally's leg. "It looks like the swelling has gone down enough that you should be able to get around with crutches. I'll drop them off this evening."

"It's only been four days," Heather reminded him as he hurried down the stairs. "Are you sure that's enough time?"

"The healing will take six to eight weeks," Dr. Evans responded, glancing at his watch, "but we want Sally to move around some on her own. Later, we'll substitute a strapped leg brace."

Dr. Evans hurried to his car, late for an appointment. Just then a car drove into the Perkins carport. "Damn," he said in a whisper, recognizing Inez Perkins. "Can't stop now. Hopefully she'll still be there tonight when I deliver Sally's crutches."

"How are you doing?" Inez asked, having phoned to check on Sally's progress.

"I'm fine," Sally responded. "I get crutches tonight."

"I hate the idea of you trying to move around on them. I never could make them work. Is the check I wrote still covering your expenses?"

"That's a question for Heather. She's in charge of bill paying, but she's downstairs at the moment."

"Please let her know there was no damage to my house during this last burglary. A few items seem to be missing, but I've notified the police and the insurance company. I just need to get the alarm system fixed again. One of its damaged parts has to be ordered, so the system won't be back in service until tomorrow."

"Will you be around long enough to stop in?"

"I don't think so. I leave again tomorrow, as soon as the alarm system is fixed."

"Let's check more clippings," Heather whispered when she returned from seeing Dr. Evans out. She put Doc Adams' box on Sally's bed and turned on the iPod pinned to the drape.

Myrtle was still in the guest room, quietly minding her own business, or at least Heather hoped that's what she was doing.

"I have some news to report." Sally spoke in low tones and reached for a pad on which she'd made notes. "Robert Perkins was a corrections officer in Idaho for five years. In 1963 Harold Adams was sentenced to ten years in that same prison, for stealing jewels. He was paroled after five years."

"Wait. Slow down." Heather grabbed her note pad and wrote: *Robert died in 1971.* "That means he was at the Idaho prison for five years before that." She looked up at Sally and smiled. "If he worked at the prison from 1966-1971 and Harold was there from 1963-1968, they were there at the same time. Their paths would have crossed one way or another."

"One more thing," Sally said. "After Robert's death his wife returned home to Idaho and worked at the prison. She left after a riot in 1973."

Heather continued making notes.

"It looks like she began using her skills as a magician after she left the prison."

Heather looked up. "That means Inez and Doc might not have met at the prison, but met later through their mutual interest in magic. What happened to her son?"

"There's a death certificate for him issued by Doernbecher Hospital in 1973. He died two years after his injuries."

It was lunchtime when Heather knocked on the door to her office, then opened it.

Myrtle was huddled on the bed looking pleased. Spread around her were tax forms. "The jailer has returned," she greeted her niece.

"You weren't locked in." Heather noticed the papers. "What are those?"

Myrtle said, "The convict wants to plea bargain. I know some of Kiki's past and it's very interesting."

Heather picked up one of the forms. "These aren't yours. They belong to Inez." She looked at Myrtle, her eyes wide and disbelieving. "You *stole* these?"

"Borrowed. I *borrowed* them. I'll give them back. And when I do, I'm going to insist on some answers."

"You can't just hand these to Inez," Heather moaned. "She trusted me with her key and I've let her down. These forms have to go back when she's out of the house."

###

With the news that the alarm system wouldn't be operational until tomorrow, Heather watched for Inez to leave on an errand. If she did, Heather would hurry over, use her key to enter, and return the *borrowed* tax forms.

Dinnertime came and went before a flash of headlights announced Inez leaving on an errand. Grabbing her key, a pen light and the tax forms, Heather rushed to Inez's back door. She unlocked it and dashed up the stairs. She had just returned the forms to the proper box when she heard a man's voice downstairs. *Had Inez returned home?*

"At last you and I are going to come to terms with what life has dealt us," the man said.

Heather froze; afraid to move for fear the creaking floor would reveal her presence. *Would Inez and her guest come upstairs? Were they lovers?* Heather huddled beside the bed, remaining as quiet as possible. If only she could get out of this situation without embarrassing herself. If it sounded like anyone left the house, she intended to be down the stairs and out the back door in a flash.

She heard the sounds of someone pulling something across the hardwood floor of the dining room.

"You'll like it best sitting in here," the man said.

What followed sounded like something being torn. *Is that material of some kind? Why isn't Inez talking?*

"I see you're finally paying attention, Ms. Perkins. Did you enjoy your little nap?"

Was the man's voice familiar?

"Now then," he said. "You have until my cigar burns down to tell me what I want to hear. After that it'll be too late."

"What could be keeping Heather?" Myrtle asked softly. "She's been gone an hour."

"Damn this broken leg. When is Dr. Evans going to show up with my crutches? He said he'd drop them off tonight."

"You couldn't go outside even if you had them. It's dark. You'd fall and break something else. Maybe Jazz showed up and Heather's with him." Myrtle sounded hopeful, but worry was etched across her forehead.

"There's certainly a way to check on that." Sally grabbed the phone and called Jazz's number.

"Yes," came a sleepy response after two rings.

"Jazz, it's Sally. You left your badge here this afternoon. Heather asked me to call and let you know where you could find it."

On the other end of the line Jazz was momentarily quiet. Finally he said, "That sister of yours is a considerate person. Put her on. I want to tell her what I think of her thoughtful reminder this late at night."

"She can't come to the phone. She's too busy, but I'll give her your message."

"Thanks, Sally. See you later!" Jazz hung up.

With five listening devices in the Samuelson house, recording every breath drawn, Sally had obviously resisted speaking outright. But, if he'd read her correctly, Heather was missing and they needed someone in an official capacity. The badge he'd supposedly left at the Samuelson house was in his pocket and his off-duty weapon was firmly in place. He was dressed and out the door in less than four minutes.

WHAT'S GOING ON?

	1	2	3	4	5	6	7	8
A	**W**	**M**	**T**	**S**	**D**	**V**	**O**	**I**
B	**R**	**C**	**P**	**B**	**M**	**G**	**K**	**E**
C	**G**	**S**	**T**	**E**	**N**	**N**	**F**	**A**
D	**R**	**E**	**R**	**F**	**O**	**L**	**U**	**R**

A2, D7, D1, A5, C4, D1,
A8, C6,
B3, D8, A7, C1, D3, B8, C2, A4

– – – – – –   – –   – – – – – – – –

CHAPTER 15

Heather could still hear the man speaking quietly. He had been threatening Inez for an hour without any verbal response from her. Couldn't she answer? Were his threats real?

Heather pictured her options. If she made an attempt to find a phone, the creaking floors would reveal her presence. If the man threatening Inez captured her before she could call 9-1-1, she wouldn't be able to rescue Inez or save herself. How responsive would neighbors be if she simply started screaming? If Vera was listening, did she understand the gravity of the situation?

"This is your last chance, Babe. This cigar is nearly gone." Inez's captor rocked back and forth in the antique rocking chair where he'd been for the last hour.

He could make out his victim's profile in the dim light. In her younger years she had undoubtedly been beautiful. Now, in her mid-fifties, all that set her apart from other women was her reputation.

He hadn't known Inez's real identity until the anonymous letter arrived. He knew now that someone else wanted her stopped. It made his personal desire to see her dead more satisfying to contemplate.

He reached in his pocket to touch one of the clippings he'd received: BOSTON BABE BAGS ANOTHER BOLD BURGLARY. That headline had made its way around the world as the adept thief, in one of her many disguises, disappeared into the noon day sun of one more country, taking with her another assortment of jewels.

A cloud of smoke was sent toward Inez. "All you have to do, Babe, is give me a sign that you're willing to trade your life for whatever's left

of the loot you've collected over the years. Nod and all will be forgiven."
It was a lie, of course, but maybe she'd fall for it.

Inez shook her head defiantly at the voice coming to her out of total darkness. She'd left on errands, then realized the letter she intended to mail was still at home. When she returned for it, she'd been struck down as she approached her front door. When she regained consciousness, she found herself gagged, blindfolded and tied to a chair. Whoever her captor was, she didn't intend to give in to his threats. In addition to being a jewel thief, she was a master magician. Surely those skills would aid her now. As quietly as possible she struggled to free herself.

Inez's captor yawned and looked at his watch. "I'm sorry to have to tell you this, Babe, but the sun will be up in a few hours. I'll have to move on before your neighbors wake up and interrupt this little tête-à-tête. It's now or never." He waited, humming bits of the song *Smoke Gets In Your Eyes*. Finally he asked, "How's your sense of smell? Can you tell your expensive scotch has been added to your drapes? Does it interest you to know that the candle I used to light my cigar is sitting beside them?" He breathed in deeply and exhaled another cloud of cigar smoke in his captive's direction. "Imagine what happens when that lit candle teams up with your alcohol-drenched drapes."

The rocking chair creaked several times as its rhythm increased with impatience. "Can't you almost feel those hungry flames licking your body?"

He watched Inez shake her head.

"So be it," he announced, getting up from the rocker. "Before I go, I'll disable your fire alarm."

Jazz arrived at the Samuelson townhouse out of breath.

"Hurry," Myrtle urged, having waited for him at the front door. "Talk to Sally."

Jazz took the stairs two at a time, and moved close to Sally as she signaled him. She whispered, "Heather left for Inez's place over an hour ago. She had a five minute errand to perform while Inez was running errands. We haven't seen her or heard from her since she left. Myrtle said Inez's car is back. We don't know if Heather's trapped there, afraid of the embarrassment of getting caught breaking in, or if something else has happened to her."

Jazz nodded and retraced his steps down the stairs and out the door.

At Inez's townhouse a man was calling softly, "Ta, ta, old woman. Last chance. The fire's already spreading. Feel the heat? I could get it under control if you give me a sign." He paused. "Still too stubborn? Too bad. Those flames will reach you within a minute or two. I'm sorry you didn't think your life was worth saving." He opened the front door and closed it quietly behind him.

Heather had listened to the man's threats, frozen in place by the ugliness of the situation. When she heard the front door open and close, she dashed downstairs. If the man came back, she'd deal with that situation then, but time was obviously running out.

"It's Heather," she whispered, pulling Inez, chair and all, back from the flames spreading up the draperies. Heather dragged the helpless woman to the safety of her kitchen. Coughing from the smoke, she grabbed Inez's radio phone and dialed 9-1-1 as one-handed, she pulled the tape from her neighbor's face.

At that moment there was pounding on the front door. Heather ran through the smoke to the door, the telephone receiver still in her hand as she answered the emergency operator's questions. "Jazz," she gasped when she'd opened the door. "Help me."

On either side of her, flames licked their way up another wall.

"Get out of the house," Jazz yelled.

"Get Inez," Heather shouted pointing toward the kitchen. She grabbed at something on an end table as she passed. "I'll warn the family next door." She raced from the house and pounded on the Keyes' door. Brad, dressed in pajamas, came to the door, then, hearing Heather's warnings, disappeared. He returned with a fire extinguisher and ran outside looking helplessly at flames creeping across furniture and drapes in his neighbor's house. When heat burst a window and Heather screamed, he trained his fire extinguisher at flaming material falling to the ground.

"Get your family out of the house," Heather yelled.

He nodded, and hurried back inside to rescue his invalid wife.

At that moment Jazz burst through the front door with Inez and her chair. He carried her to the carport where Heather waited.

"As you arrived, did you see anyone leaving?" Heather asked.

"A Mercedes was pulling away." He eased the last restraint from Inez. "What's this all about?"

Heather whispered, "A murder attempt." She looked at her neighbor. "Do you need to go to the hospital?"

Inez coughed several times, but shook her head. She wiggled her arms and shoulders, working out the stiffness caused by her hours of confinement. Then she took a step and fell.

Jazz grabbed her.

"Who did this to you?" Heather asked.

Again Inez shook her head. She started to speak, then coughed. "I don't know. He said he'd taken things from my house yesterday. That's all I know."

Jazz looked at the woman. "If he got everything yesterday, why did he come back today?"

###

"Sally," Myrtle shouted from downstairs. "There's a fire at Kiki's." The reflection from the burning building was turning night into day.

"Are we in danger?"

"Not yet," Myrtle yelled back. "Get dressed in case we have to evacuate."

Sally reached for her clothes on the chair next to her bed.

"I'll check on things and get back to you." Myrtle rushed out the door as flashing lights and sirens announced the arrival of fire trucks and police. She could see flames shooting out of heat-shattered windows. Myrtle twisted her hands nervously. Was Heather trapped inside? What about Kiki? And Jazz? Where had Jazz gone?

Before long the fire was under control, except for bits of smoldering wood pulled from the house. Firemen took precautions as they checked for hotspots needing attention.

"Tape the area." The command came from the fire marshal as he stepped from the house, an empty alcohol bottle in his gloved hand.

WHO WAS THAT MASKED MAN?

J + 4 =	V - 2 =	K + 1 =	L + 6 =
J + 5 =	G + 1 =	S - 4 =	E - 4 =
P + 4 =	A + 4 =	O - 1 =	H + 6 =
		B + 3 =	C + 4 =
		K - 6 =	
		T - 2 =	

_ _ _   _ _ _   _ _ _ _   _ _ _ _ _ _

CHAPTER 16

At the Samuelson house Inez showered and tried to wash the smell of smoke from her hair. Warm tea, Myrtle's extra pajamas, and the Samuelson's hide-a-bed awaited her.

Jazz had consulted with the police and the fire marshal, and they agreed to hold off talking to Inez until morning. After he took the listening devices from the living room and dining room and put them in the kitchen, he carried Sally downstairs to take part in the discussion.

"I think I need to speak first, Kiki," Myrtle said. She wrapped her arm around her friend. "I stole the key you left with Heather."

Inez looked at her friend and smiled. "That makes it almost like old times, doesn't it?"

Myrtle nodded. "I went into your house and found your income tax forms. I stole two of them." Myrtle blushed. "Heather was very upset with me, but I needed to know why you were pretending to be someone else when we could be having good times together."

"What gave me away?" Inez asked.

"The moles." Myrtle laughed as Inez's hand brushed her neck. "I remembered the six moles."

Heather interrupted. "I was embarrassed that I hadn't protected the items you trusted me with. I wanted to return the forms Aunt Myrtle took without admitting she'd stolen them. I knew your alarm wasn't working, so when you left on errands, I hurried over. I'd just returned the forms when I heard a voice downstairs. I was afraid to move in case your floors creaked like ours do. I couldn't figure any way out of the house without letting you know I was there."

"It's a good thing you were there," Inez said, coughing again. She smiled at Heather. "If you hadn't been, I'd be Melba toast now."

Heather returned her smile. "All this time we've been trying to figure out why you stopped being Kiki. Then I heard that man call you Boston Babe. Where does that name come from?"

"Boston Babe?" Jazz and Myrtle spoke simultaneously.

Jazz looked suspiciously at Heather's neighbor. "Is that who you are?"

Myrtle was laughing. "So that's how you became famous. I've read about you in newspapers."

Inez smiled at her friend, then looked at the deputy. "If you're familiar with that name and I admit that's who I am, will you arrest me?"

"You need to be careful what you tell us or admit to; the statute of limitations may not apply."

Inez nodded. "For Myrtle's sake I'll go back to the year I graduated."

"1965," supplied Myrtle.

Inez continued, "I met Robert Perkins shortly after I graduated. He was attending the police academy in Boston." She paused, "He was a very special man, and I loved him dearly.

"Our son Kevin was born two years later." She smiled fondly at the picture Heather had saved from the fire. "We were vacationing in Detroit in 1971, because Robert had family there. He took Kevin with him to the jewelry trade fair because he intended to buy a birthday present for me. The trade fair was a big event. Craftsmen from all over the world were there."

Inez cleared her throat. "At first, it was the sound of breaking glass that alerted people. They said it sounded like picture windows shattering. Three men in sports apparel were smashing display cases and scooping out jewels. The sales staff hid under the display tables. Not one of them called for help or assisted customers, so it was easy for the thieves to take what they'd come for."

Tears caught Inez by surprise as she spoke. "Robert was carrying Kevin so he could see the displays. When things started happening, someone pushed Robert into a display case. It shattered and he and Kev received deep cuts. Robert tried to stem the flow of blood from Kev's neck wound, but by the time someone called 9-1-1 and paramedics reached my baby, Kev was near death and Robert couldn't be helped.

Kev survived for two years, in a vegetative state. I got him home to Idaho, then transferred him to Doernbecher Hospital in Portland.

"I was so bitter there weren't words to express how I felt. If the cowardly sales staff had provided better security in the first place, the theft wouldn't have happened in broad daylight. And if they hadn't spent all those precious minutes hiding under tables and had assisted Robert . . . ." Her voice broke.

"I vowed on my son's grave I'd make them pay." She looked at her audience. There were tears in Heather's eyes and Myrtle was sobbing quietly. Jazz and Sally watched with sad expressions.

"And so, I leaned back on a former skill and after attending classes became a master magician. Other than magic lessons I learned about what's being called *distraction' robberies*." She turned to Myrtle. "Do you remember that watch I came home with the first time we tried on everything that Boston jeweler had?"

Myrtle smiled and nodded.

"I got a whole lot better at doing that."

"And that's how Boston Babe came to be?" asked Heather.

"That's it. No weapons, no scaring anyone half to death with threats. I just walked in and after a while walked out with something valuable. There has never been anyone yelling *stop thief* and I only *shopped* at dealers who were at the Detroit jewelry fair that year. My courier job sends me around the world, so visiting those dealers has been easy."

"Did any of your visits include Coffman Jewelers?" Heather asked.

Inez looked at Heather. "Maybe."

"Then the ring Dr. Evans thought resembled one being crafted for his fiancé could have been the ring you were wearing."

"It was a mistake wearing it to the hospital, but of course when I put it on that morning I had no plans to be anywhere near a hospital. Why I had to run into the one person who would recognize it . . . ." Her voice trailed off. "If that answers most of your questions, then I'd like to sleep now. I guess I'm more shaken than I thought. Tomorrow I'll have to meet with the police and fire investigators."

"But you haven't told us what tonight's escapade was all about," Sally said.

"I think Heather can fill you in on that. I'd really like to rest."

"Before you do, I have a question," Jazz said. "Should we call you Inez or Kiki?"

"Kiki died when Kev did. I'm Inez."

"Well then, Inez, do you have any idea who tried to murder you tonight?"

"I have no idea who he was, but if I never again hear *Smoke Gets in Your Eyes*, it will be too soon."

###

With Inez fast asleep, the others moved to Sally's bedroom so Heather could relay what she'd overheard.

"Do you have any idea who the man was?" asked Jazz.

"I didn't see him; I only heard his voice, but I know of at least two possibilities." She told them of eavesdropping on the conversation between Inez and Dr. Evans and the ring that had changed the course of the doctor's life. "Dr. Evans was supposed to bring Sally's crutches tonight, but he hasn't come. He drives a Mercedes."

"Do you think he places that much value on a ring?"

"I think he places that much value on the life he planned which the stolen ring made impossible. Another person I'm curious about is Abe Coffman." Heather repeated what the manager at Worldwide had said concerning a man asking questions about Inez. Heather felt sure the description fit the short jeweler. It was almost certain that Inez had stolen jewelry from Abe Coffman.

"Anything else?" Jazz asked.

"When I was with Abe recently, he commented on the blue van in our carport."

"Why did he care about that?" asked Sally.

"Apparently he checks our carport every day as he drives past Taborhill to and from his shop."

"Strange," Jazz mused. "Your carport isn't on the way from Abe's home to his shop."

###

Myrtle went to bed and Jazz headed back to his apartment to finish his interrupted night's sleep. Heather and Sally set Doc Adams' box of clippings between them. With Inez's confession, the stories Doc saved were bound to make more sense. As for listening devices, two were now in the kitchen with the remainder in Heather's bedroom.

"Look at this 1962 article about a jewel theft," Heather said. "It has H.A. penciled at the top. I think Doc pulled that robbery and labeled this with his initials."

"And?"

"And if he and Inez were both magicians, and she wanted revenge on those jewelers, I think Doc taught her more than magic tricks. At least that would make sense out of what Jake overheard. Doc taught other magicians how to rob, but except for Inez, the others have been less successful. They obviously didn't have *good hands.*"

###

The morning Clarion carried a brief story regarding a house fire at Taborhill Garden Estates at eleven o'clock the previous evening.

"That bumbler," grumped Joel Bishop's hit man. "We hand him the Boston Babe and he botches it."

"What do you want to do now?"

"What we should have done in the first place. Take care of Babe ourselves."

"Are you still waiting for her to come to you?"

"Now that we know her real name and where she lives, we don't have to wait. Anything that happens to her will be blamed on that idiot who didn't have the guts to cut her throat before he started the fire."

###

"Heather, it's Rachel. Are you all right? Is your house close to the one that burned? Do you need me to help with anything?"

"Calm down, Sis. We're fine. The fire wasn't even close to us. Remind me when you're leaving for Baltimore."

"Jason's conference is Monday. We're going the day before."

"Whoa! You leave in two days? Are you packed? Do you need anyone to take care of plants?"

"It's all under control. I'll see you when we get back."

When Jazz went to work the next morning, he planned to tell Sergeant Miller of the previous evening's events. But Ox, preparing for retirement the end of December, had the day off. With no one to talk to, Jazz began researching Abe Coffman's background and the history of Coffman Jewelers.

Names were funny. Some popped up everywhere you looked—on buildings, street signs, ads. If Ox Miller had been on duty, Jazz would have laughingly pointed out that in 1969 Isaac Coffman started out as a partner in Coffman and Miller, Jewelers. They'd been in business for two years when the Detroit robbery took place and forced them to declare bankruptcy. Eventually, Coffman and Miller returned to the business world only as Coffman.

Ox would get a kick out of knowing someone named Miller had been a jeweler. Jazz looked forward to kidding him. It might be interesting to see if the early Miller actually was a relative. If he was, Ox might not take kindly to kidding. Armed with good intentions, Jazz began researching the background of former jeweler, R.C. Miller.

When Heather awoke, she found their houseguest gone. She waited until lunch time, but Inez didn't return or call. When the fire inspectors arrived on the scene, Heather wandered back to the burned house to view the damage.

Luckily, the fire had been limited to the living room and dining room where floors, walls and furniture took the brunt of the incident. Ceilings were scorched, but hadn't burned enough to spread the fire to the second floor. Adding to the damage was that of water hoses dragged through the rooms.

While Heather looked at the damage done to Inez's home, Inez walked briskly along a Lewisburg street, looking in store windows as she made her way to Coffman Jewelers.

"Good day, Sir." Abe Coffman greeted the customer who entered his shop. He rose from his work station, setting aside intricate pieces he'd been working on. He reached for his jacket, nursing a small cut to his right hand. The missing joints of his index finger made handling the drill awkward. "May I help you with something?"

Today's customer wore a gray beret, a suede jacket, and trousers with knife-sharp pleats. The man coughed several times before he said, "I gotta stop smoking. It's killing my throat." The customer's gruff voice grated like sandpaper.

Abe inhaled, then coughed. The smell clinging to the man confirmed him as a heavy smoker.

"My sweetheart has a birthday next week," the customer said. "I want something special because I plan on proposing. I've been to most of your competitors but they don't have anything that's special enough."

"I'm sure I can satisfy your needs," Abe said. "Do you have something specific in mind or a price range?"

"She already has a Rolex. I gave her that for Valentine's Day. For Easter I gave her a diamond the size of Liz Taylor's."

Abe was salivating.

"There must be something I can surprise her with. I'll leave it to you to show me what you'd offer the most wonderful woman alive if she was your woman."

Abe gestured toward expensive pins.

"Thanks." Abe's customer coughed again. "That's not special enough. I'll keep looking. I want something that will take Rena's breath away." He started for the door.

"Sir," Abe called. "I have one item I only show my best customers." Abe had turned to his safe and was spinning the dial. In a moment the expensive box containing the Duchess Diamonds rested on the counter. "I don't allow customers to touch these diamonds," Abe cautioned, "but you can look."

Inez sucked in her breath, coughing several more times. The diamonds she'd been searching for were even more lustrous than she'd been led to believe. "I think that's exactly what Rena deserves. She'd feel like a princess wearing those." Abe's customer laughed. "Now *there's* an idea! Do you have anything that resembles a tiara? Every princess needs one of those to wear when she unwraps a gift like those diamonds. If you have tiaras, let me look at them."

Abe reached under the counter as Inez snapped shut the lid of the expensive box.

"Don't you want to put these gems back in your safe while I look at tiaras? We don't want too many things out at one time."

Abe nodded and put the box in the safe, then lifted tiaras to the counter. Three were lined up. Inez pointed to the most expensive one as a customer, running errands on a busy lunch hour, burst in.

"Came by to pick up my watch if you've got it repaired, Abe."

"Be right with you, Barney," Abe responded, turning back to his customer to quote a price for the diamonds and the tiara.

"Add that tiara to the safe with the diamonds. I don't want you selling them before I get back with the cash. I don't like to carry that much money so I'll get a cashier's check. Will that be acceptable?"

Abe nodded. He was almost drooling as he added the tiara to the safe. He turned as Inez doffed the beret, then reached out to shake Abe's hand. "I'll be back in ten, maybe fifteen minutes."

The jeweler could hardly believe his good fortune. With the sale of the Duchess Diamonds and a tiara, Coffman Jewelers would just about be operating on its own again, instead of on the contract money he was earning with his sideline. Of course, the diamonds would have to be treated to destroy bacteria meant to eventually put a painful end to the Boston Babe. Delighted beyond reason, Abe located the repaired watch for his friend.

Also congratulating herself on her good fortune was the Boston Babe. Nestled under the doffed beret were the Duchess Diamonds. She could hardly wait to show them to Doc Adams.

###

It had been almost an hour since Abe Coffman's customer left to get a cashier's check. Abe was getting anxious. Could the man be having trouble freeing up that much cash?

When two hours went by and the customer hadn't called to explain the delay, Abe allowed himself to become suspicious. Laughing at his fears, he opened the safe and then the expensive box used to display the Duchess Diamonds.

He gasped. The box was empty. Abe collapsed in a chair. Coffman Jewelers would be ruined. He'd have to declare bankruptcy. Even the contract millions for his sideline wouldn't bail him out of this hole.

It had to be the Boston Babe who'd taken them. Could the man looking for a gift for his lover have been Babe in disguise? Abe shook his head. Whoever made off with the diamonds would become international news within a day or two because of the anthrax spores he'd deposited on them. Cutaneous anthrax took one to six days to germinate and release toxic substances. These substances caused internal bleeding, swelling and tissue death. Abe hummed to himself as he retrieved one of the surveillance tapes so he could view the theft taking place. The thief's painful death would be a fitting punishment for his crime.

CHAPTER 17

When a Mercedes pulled into the Samuelson carport that evening, Heather met its driver at the door.

"Sorry I couldn't get here last night," Dr. Evans apologized, crutches in one hand. "I had an emergency. Let's see how these babies fit Sally." Heather followed him as they climbed the stairs to Sally's room. "How're you doing?" he asked his patient. "Ready to give crutches a try?"

"You bet." Sally tossed back her covers, swinging her legs to the side.

Dr. Evans assisted her in standing, adjusted a hand grip on the crutches, and watched her attempt a few steps.

"These really work," Sally said. "Thanks for bringing them by."

Dr. Evans wished her well and headed back to his car with Heather following. "Did you hear about our neighbor's fire last night?" she asked.

"I saw something about a house fire in the paper this morning. Apparently no one was injured."

"The fireman got there fast enough to save Mrs. Perkins."

Dr. Evans laughed. "Perkins, huh? It sounds like the Samuelson curse has definitely spawned the Perkins curse." He moved in the direction of the fire-damaged building. "Why's the yellow tape around everything?"

"The arson squad is investigating."

"Arson squad?"

"I guess they have to rule it out," Heather responded.

Inez's front door hung from one hinge. Dr. Evans peeked in. "She's lucky," he said. "It looks like it got pretty hot in there. Where was she when the fire broke out?"

"I don't know," Heather lied. "I suppose, based on the time of day, she must have been in bed."

Dr. Evans nodded, then headed back to the Samuelson carport. "Tell Sally I'll check on her progress with the crutches in a day or two. I get to take this weekend off so I'm going hunting." He looked happy.

Heather stood by as he opened his car door and got in. He was doing some off-key humming as the door closed behind him. The expression on Heather's face turned to horror as the vehicle departed.

Dr. Evans had been humming *Smoke Gets In Your Eyes* and it sounded all too familiar.

Hammering the next morning woke several of the Perkins' neighbors.

"What's going on?" asked Sally, making her first attempt at stepping outside with the crutches.

"They're nailing a large sheet of plywood over Inez's front door," Heather said. "She tucked a note under my windshield wipers. Worldwide Courier wants her to make a delivery in Singapore."

"They keep her busy. What's happening with that street light near her house?"

Heather looked out the door. "Looks like it's being worked on again. Brad's there. I'll get details and let you know." Heather headed down the street to the corner where Brad stood beside a ladder. At the top an electrician was at work. "I see you've hired a new company to work on the problems."

"We've gotta get the light working," he responded.

"Hey, fella," called the electrician near the top of the ladder. "Who've you been hiring?"

"Aba Brothers Electrical," Brad called back.

"You may have cause to sue them." The electrician climbed down. Wires and metal parts were in his hand.

"Why's that?" Brad asked.

"This is a heat sensor. When the temperature inside the light fixture reaches a certain temperature this baby turns the light off. But, since you've got a solar mechanism that recognizes darkness, after things cool down, that mechanism turns the light back on."

"You've gotta be kidding me? I didn't know they could do something like that."

Heather looked at Brad. "Do you think Leonardo wired the lamp like that?"

"He may not have, but he certainly should have discovered the problem," Brad said.

"If Leonardo rigged the light to turn off and on, did he do it so he could break into houses on your street?" Could it have been Leonardo who tried to murder Inez? How soon before Inez returned from Singapore?

Heather called the manager of Worldwide Courier and Delivery as soon as she got home.

"She didn't go," the manager replied. "She took the week off. There was a death in her family."

Heather hung up. If Inez didn't leave town, why hadn't she been in touch? Was Boston Babe at it again? If so, where would she go? Heather gasped. The Duchess Diamonds! They'd been displayed on the internet. Would that tempt her?

"Jazz," Heather said, when her call was answered. "You wanted to know more about what happened to Inez the other night, and I want to know more about something else. If you pick me up we can trade information."

"Does this mean you want to meet for coffee?"

"That and taking a peek at engagement rings." Heather was laughing even before she hung up.

"I'm disappointed," Jazz said, maneuvering his car into downtown Lewisburg. "I thought your reference to an engagement ring meant you were going to propose to me."

Heather smiled. "Sorry, Jazz. You're going with me undercover."

When Jazz leered at her, she added, "Be serious. We're going to see if Boston Babe is back at work."

"If she is, won't the jeweler she robs call it in?" He swerved to avoid a jaywalker.

"That's what we're going to find out. Stop in the next block."

Jazz parked in front of Coffman Jewelers. "What's my part in this?"

"You want to buy the most expensive piece of jewelry in the shop. It's to be my engagement present."

"Not going to be satisfied with the usual ring?"

Heather smiled, took his arm and marched him into Abe's shop.

"Miss Heather," Abe Coffman greeted. "Not any problems with the website, are there? I'm getting some nice offers to purchase various pieces."

"No website problems," Heather answered, directing an adoring gaze up at Jazz.

Picking up on his cue, Jazz reminded Abe they'd met before, but added, "This trip is my doing, Mr. Coffman. Heather has promised to marry me and . . . ."

"Congratulations," Abe said, moving to the display of diamond rings. "Let's check the lady's ring size. Give me your left hand, Heather." Abe measured Heather's finger size while Jazz looked at rings. "Find anything that appeals to you, sir?"

"I think my girl has her eye on something she's seen here before. Speak up, Heather. Point it out."

"Abe, I'd like Jazz to see the Duchess Diamonds."

Jazz slipped his arm around Heather and leaned down to plant a quick kiss on top of her head.

Abe pulled out a picture. "This is what they look like," he said. "You'll note the price listed below."

Jazz read the price and turned pale.

Heather said, "Let's show him the real thing." She was pointing at his wall safe.

Abe ducked his head. "I can't do that, Heather. The diamonds are on loan."

"On loan? Did you send them to a museum? What if you get an offer for them?"

"Then I'll ask for them back," Abe said. "Why not select a ring? There are several very nice ones."

Heather said, "I don't want to make my selection until Jazz sees your *piece de resistance*. When he sees that, he'll be relieved when I pick out something with only a few diamonds clustered all over it." She brushed at her hair, and reached for Jazz's arm again.

"I should have the Duchess Diamonds back by the end of next week," Abe said. "Stop in again Thursday or Friday."

"Can't do that, Abe," Heather said with a little wave. "How about the week after that?"

"Are you two headed some special place? Maybe a nice beach with mai tai's on the tray beside you?" Abe watched them carefully.

"My design company requires attention," Heather volunteered.

"It's okay. You don't have to tell me where you're going."

As they left the shop Jazz asked, "Did we learn what you wanted to know?"

Heather nodded. "I don't think the Duchess Diamonds are on loan. I think Babe has them. Abe didn't show them because he couldn't."

"If they've been stolen, why not report the theft?" Jazz unlocked Heather's car door.

"I don't know the answer, but it has to be for a really good reason." She ducked her head and settled in the passenger seat.

"Have you heard any more from Inez?"

"Nothing, and her boss said she asked for a week's vacation because of a death in her family. Of course we know she doesn't *have* any family."

Jazz walked around the car and got in. "What about the trip you're taking this weekend? You were careful not to tell Abe where you were headed. Care to tell me?"

Heather said, "I'll just be gone a day or two."

Jazz looked at her suspiciously. Generally Heather was open with him. There was only one subject she kept close to her chest. "Does this trip you aren't telling me about have anything to do with your mom's scrapbook?"

Heather looked startled. "N-no," she stuttered.

Jazz laughed as he started the car. He began singing, "*Your lips tell me no, no, but there's yes, yes in your eyes.*"

"*If Babe took the bait, then why are you leaving town later in the week?*" the assassin's accomplice asked.

"*That Samuelson girl is headed out of town. She was careful not to say where she's going. People always want to brag about their destinations, even if it's a business trip.*"

"So? Who cares where she's headed?"

"It's September. Maybe she's taking over annual visits to see her dad."

"Instead of her mom taking those trips, you mean? Too bad we didn't discover those trips sooner."

"Right. I have a pal in security at PDX. I'll see if he can find out where Heather's headed. Maybe I'll be taking a short vacation too, and maybe one of us won't come home."

"Let me know what you find out. I'm anxious to get that thieving Charlie Samuelson taken care of."

###

When Heather got home she found Sally downstairs, happily hobbling about on her crutches.

"I've got some news for you," Sally said.

The listening devices in Heather's bedroom and in the kitchen were transmitting music from a local radio station.

Heather settled on the sofa. "Let's trade information—you first."

"Myrtle and I finished looking through Doc's clippings. They are all about jewel thefts around the world, each with what we think are initials of perpetrators penciled somewhere on the article. A lot with BB begin showing up. We're betting that's for Boston Babe."

"Perfect. I think we need to check on Doc's health and decide whether to tell Father Raymond about his dad's jail time in case they need to chat about it."

"That's the other news," Sally said. "Father Raymond called. His dad died yesterday."

Heather looked startled, then jumped to her feet. "That's it! That's the *death in the family* Inez told her boss at Worldwide about. Did Father Raymond mention Inez?"

"No."

"I'll bet she's there." Heather headed for the door.

"Wait," called Sally. "You didn't tell me your news."

###

STORY STEW

Re-arrange the letters to form words with a common theme.

D E E M R R U R	E I N O O P S R	G I L T U Y
A I N O R S S T	E F L N O Y	C D E E E N N S T
E F H I T	C D E H I I M O	A C I I L M N R

CHAPTER 18

Heather hurried to The Boardwalk to talk to Jake. She thought he might have overheard news of Inez, or her plans.

The nurse in charge seemed pleased that she'd stopped. "I hoped you'd come. I only wish you could have been here yesterday before Doc died. He'd been quite lucid these last couple of days and in good spirits." She put one chart aside and reached for another.

"Was Father Raymond with his dad when he died?"

"No. Just his personal physician. First time in twelve years we've seen that rascal."

Heather's eyes were wide. "You've only seen Doc's primary care doctor once in twelve years? Who's his doctor? I want to avoid him."

"Let me think." Nurse Kinder was chewing on her pencil. "Bevans. He said his name was Bevans."

"How about Evans. Could he have said Evans?"

"Could have. I was getting meds ready when he stopped and asked directions to Doc's room. I had my mind on the meds and he said he didn't need me to assist with anything."

"Could I talk with Jake, please?"

"You can try. Doc's death affected him badly. We had to move him to a new room while we cleaned up. Jake's across the hall from 465."

"Thanks," Heather said, heading down the hall.

She stepped into Jake's new room and gasped. "Are you all right?"

"'Course I'm all right. It's these idiot nurses who aren't tracking clearly." He struggled against straps around his wrists, tying his arms to the bed frames.

"Why are you in restraints?" Heather settled in the chair beside his bed.

"'Cause no one will believe me when I tell them what I saw. They keep telling me I imagined it."

"What is it you saw that no one will believe?"

"Saw what that man visiting Doc did. He said he was a doctor, but doctors don't kill people. They make them get better."

"Doc's visitor killed him? How?"

"Held a pillow over his face until Doc stopped kicking and sucking in air."

"Why would he do that?" Heather unwrapped a mint.

"'Cause Doc wouldn't tell him what he wanted to know. That murderer was asking about some woman and Doc wouldn't tell him. He just kept laughing."

"Do you remember the woman's name? Was it Inez? Kiki? Boston Babe?"

"Two 'a those. The baby and the kitten."

"Babe and Kiki?"

"That's what I said."

"Why didn't he kill you if you saw what he did?"

"I think he might have 'cept I pretended to be asleep and had my call button in my hand, under the covers. Kept pushing it. That big nurse came rushing in and that's when the murderer said Doc had just stopped breathing. I yelled. Told her what he'd done to Doc. She wouldn't believe me. Not after that murderer said it was Doc's dying that put me out of my head and she needed to tie me to the bed so I didn't hurt myself. Then that murdering sums-a-bitch smiled all happy-like and left."

Heather fed Jake a mint. She was thinking of a murderer with a cigar who hummed *Smoke Gets in Your Eyes*. Was her long-time physician that person? He'd said he was going hunting. Was it Inez he was hunting?

"Jake, I'm going to ask a favor of you. Nod if you understand me. Don't try to talk with that mint in your mouth. Do you understand so far?" Heather waited for a response.

Jake nodded vigorously.

"Here's what I want you to do. Keep what the murderer did a secret. Don't tell anyone. I know two cops really well and I'm going to talk to them. If you stop trying to get other people to believe you, Nurse

Kinder will stop restraining you. Can you do that? Can you trust me to see that the murderer gets what's coming to him?"

Jake nodded again.

"Don't forget. This is our secret, yours and mine. It might take us a day or two, but we're going to get that killer put behind bars."

"Sums-a-bitch, thass who he is."

"I'm glad you stopped by," Nurse Kinder said as Heather prepared to leave. "Will you be seeing Father Raymond any time soon?"

"I'm headed there now."

"Could you take this paper to him? We found it under Doc's mattress when we cleaned his room. It's just a list of names and doesn't look very important, but as long as you're going to see him . . . ."

"I'll be glad to take it." Heather reached for the paper and tucked it in a pocket. "Jake's quite lucid now," she reported.

"Really? He didn't try to tell you a doctor murdered Doc Adams?"

"Is that what he's been saying?" Heather asked. "He hardly mentioned Doc and was more interested in the mints I brought along. I have a few more he could have if you'd untie him so he can get the papers off." She handed the mints to Nurse Kinder. "Was the personal physician Doc's only visitor yesterday?"

"No. There was another man here for a while. He came early and really cheered Doc up. I've never heard Doc laugh so much."

"Do you know the visitor's name?"

"No, but Doc kept calling him Duchess. I always thought that was a girl's name."

Heather stopped to see Father Raymond and give him the paper Nurse Kinder had found.

"I already have a copy of that," he said. "Those are the names of Dad's students from the magic school."

"May I keep this copy?" Heather asked.

"Of course. By the way, I'm having a small service for Dad after church tomorrow. I hope you'll come."

Heather nodded. She expected Inez to be at the memorial service. It was time the two of them had a serious talk.

Jazz joined the Samuelsons for dinner that evening, eager to tell of the visit to the jeweler. Heather explained her reason for going there and her suspicions regarding Babe's activity. She reminded everyone that Dr. Evans had promised to deliver Sally's crutches the night of the fire, but hadn't. Then she reported on her conversation with Jake Lundeen.

Jazz said. "If Jake is right and Dr. Evans killed Doc Adams, we need to get some hard evidence against him. Is there any?"

"Only circumstantial evidence and suspicions," Heather said. "I think he brought Sally's crutches right on schedule, but detoured to Inez's place. Unfortunately, I never saw the man who tried to kill her."

"Fingerprints," suggested Sally. "We know the arson squad will be checking for those. Maybe he left some on that empty alcohol bottle they found."

"But the doctor's prints won't be in their data bank. We'll have to get them some way," Heather said.

"If you find the doctor isn't the guilty party, you'll need another suspect. Do you have one?" Myrtle asked.

"There's another possibility," Heather said, and told them of Leonardo's off-again, on-again, light fixture.

Sally asked, "Has anyone talked to him?"

"Not yet," Heather said. "But I will. And the next time Dr. Evans checks on you, Sally, ask him to hand you something. A glass of water, maybe. Something we can get his fingerprints on."

"I'd like to change the subject," Jazz said. "I want somebody to tell me about this trip Heather's taking."

"You told him?" Sally looked surprised. "I thought we agreed to keep it a secret?"

"What trip?" Myrtle cut in. "No one told me you were taking a trip." She looked from Sally to Heather.

"When, Heather?" Jazz asked. "And where?"

"I can't tell you," Heather replied, explaining to Sally how the subject had come up while at Coffman Jewelers.

"I'm going with you, Heather," Jazz said. "So you might as well tell me. As you pointed out when you discovered the listening devices, you may have given the bad guys the time and place. They might be waiting for you. I want to make sure the bait, that's you, isn't in the way of stray bullets."

After Father Raymond's church service the next day, there was a small gathering of Doc's friends. Knowing that Inez liked to be in disguise, Heather paid close attention to the mourners, both male and female.

"Hi, Heather," called Jake when patients from The Boardwalk arrived. He maneuvered his wheelchair to Heather's side, then spotted Dr. Evans, and nearly forgot his pledge.

Heather sat beside him, holding his hands. As she did, she angled her body so she could keep an eye on Dr. Evans in case he recognized Inez before she did.

The memorial service began with the organist playing Doc's favorite hymn. Heather admired the adept hand movements over the keys, then realized the organist's hands were covered with fine scratches and cuts. She couldn't see the musician's face, but she was sure Inez was the organist.

When the music ended, Father Raymond greeted his father's friends individually and let them talk of their times with his father. As the service came to a close, he asked Heather to remain for a few minutes. Dr. Evans exchanged greetings with her, but left when the others did. As the organist collected music and prepared to leave, Heather blocked the way.

"We need to talk," Heather whispered. "I think I know who tried to murder you."

"I know, too," came the whispered response, "but I don't know how to prove it."

"Sally and I are working on a way to get Dr. Evans' fingerprints so they can be compared with those on the empty scotch bottle the murderer handled."

"Dr. Evans? No, that's not who wants me dead."

"But he killed Doc Adams because Doc wouldn't tell him how to find you. Jake saw Dr. Evans hold a pillow over Doc's face. He said Doc just kept laughing and mumbling *Duchess*."

Inez ducked her head, a shocked expression on her face.

"You stole the Duchess Diamonds, didn't you?"

Inez didn't answer. Instead she rubbed the backs of her hands.

Heather noticed the scratches again. "You got those when you tried to untie yourself. They look more like small blisters now."

"They seem to be infected."

"You should see a doctor."

"Who do you suggest? Dr. Evans? What if you're right? What if he's the person who tried to kill me?"

"There are other doctors in town. See one of them."

"I'll consider it," Inez said, moving away as Father Raymond approached.

"My dad asked me to give you this," he said to Heather, handing her a book. "I think he hoped you'd give it to Inez. It was one of Dad's favorites."

The book was titled, *Turning Straw into Gold—Rapunzel's Secret*.

###

THE SEARCH CONTINUES

Search for the little word that fits within the bigger word.
Use each little word only once.
An arsonist rests among them.

ACE, EAR, EGO, FIN, HOP, LIE, OUR, VAN, WAR

F _ _ _ R	P L _ _ _ S	S _ _ _ P E R
E _ _ _ S	S _ _ _ C H	S _ _ _ C E
R E _ _ _ E	O R _ _ _ N	A _ _ _ D

CHAPTER 19

"Any chance our paths will cross this next week?" Rachel asked Heather. Jason was loading the family car, ready for the drive to Portland International.

"I doubt it," Heather replied. "Jason will be attending business meetings in Baltimore and Washington, D.C. while you and the boys go sightseeing. And I don't even arrive until the fifteenth. Where I'm headed is off your route, and I expect to be there only one day."

"Then where will you go?" Rachel asked.

"I have no idea. I haven't purchased a round trip ticket because I don't know when I'll return."

"I wish you weren't going alone."

"I'll be fine," Heather assured her. "Stay in touch with Sally."

Heather hung up the phone; then rushed to the box of clippings that once belonged to Doc Adams. She pulled out his list of students and studied the names. Sure enough, Tom, Dick and Harvey—the Jenkins brothers—were listed. And S.J.? Heather glanced at the list again. How about Seth Jones?

She congratulated herself. Doc's box of clippings wasn't just a collection of stories about jewel thefts. He was tracking the accomplishments of his students.

###

It was late Sunday when Abe again viewed the surveillance tape showing his diamonds being palmed. He studied the technique. The thief's hand with the diamonds went to the beret where, as the cap was doffed, the diamonds were slipped into its lining.

Smooth. Very smooth.

Abe took a swig of Scotch, marveling at the ease with which the diamonds disappeared. He absent-mindedly scratched an itchy place on his right hand and turned the tape back to the beginning to watch the clever theft take place once more.

He could see what looked like fine scratches on the thief's hands, and it made him laugh. Abe's contacts overseas had promised to send fast-acting bacteria from the disease's eighty-nine known strains. If any of the thief's scratches came in contact with the spores painted on the diamonds, the thief would quickly become infected. Bacteria would travel through his bloodstream, multiplying at a rapid rate.

What should he do next? Warn the hospital of a possible case? Would the telltale red Adams-spots that blistered and hardened as their ulcerated centers became blood-tinged craters be recognized for what they were? Perhaps a better plan was to wait for the thief to show up, too ill to recover. Abe smirked and reached again for the Scotch as the tape continued.

He filled his glass, picked it up, then glanced back at the tape. The glass he held slipped through his fingers and crashed to the floor. In a daze he started the tape again, watching breathlessly as the scene repeated.

The thief was right-handed. The diamonds had been lifted from their case with the right hand. It was also the thief's right hand that doffed the beret, tucked the bacteria-coated diamonds into its lining, and then reached out—to shake Abe's right hand.

He looked down at the itchy spot he'd been scratching. It had once been a minor injury caused by a drill bit. Could the bacterium from the thief's hand have transferred to his cut? It had been two days already. Could he take the chance he hadn't been infected? He looked at the itchy spot again. Who would treat him and not report the problem?

In a panic, Abe considered his only possibility.

###

Dr. Weston Evans had Sunday off. He'd gone to the memorial service of the old guy he'd smothered, hoping Inez would be there, but he hadn't seen her. He wanted his ring back. He wanted Mary Ellen back. He wanted the life he'd been missing out on restored.

He didn't know how many times he could stop at Sally Samuelson's, pretending to be concerned about her leg, without his trips raising suspicion. Doctor's didn't make house calls any more, but her leg was his only excuse for being anywhere close to Inez Perkins. He was sitting in his Mercedes contemplating various options when his cell phone rang. "Yah," he barked, wishing he'd turned off the phone.

"Dr. Evans!" It was a nurse at the hospital. "We have a patient in emergency who refuses to see any doctor except you. He's also refusing to tell us what his problem is."

"It's my day off. Tell him to come back tomorrow; I'll see him then."

"You don't understand," the nurse said. "He's making threats. He said that if you don't treat him right now he's prepared to share his health problem with millions of innocent people who will die from it. Can't you come in just for a few minutes? He may have infected the entire emergency room staff."

Frowning, Dr. Evans said, "Okay. I'm coming." He turned off his cell phone and headed back to the hospital.

"He's in there." The excited nurse pointed to an enclosed area. "We thought it sounded like he had something contagious."

Dr. Evans recognized Abe Coffman. He was pacing back and forth like a caged animal.

"Do you want me to go in with you? Should I call security?" the nurse asked.

"I'll be all right," Dr. Evans replied. "I know him. He's a local jeweler who did some work for me a long time ago." Dr. Evans entered the enclosed space and extended his hand to be shaken.

"You won't want to do that, Doc," Abe said, keeping his gloved hands to himself. "First off, close that door. Then you and I are going to establish some facts since we have something in common." Abe sat down and pointed to a chair. Dr. Evans closed the door and sat down as directed.

"You got a letter in the mail last week—anonymously. It told you where you'd find the thief who stole that engagement ring I was making for you."

"You sent that letter?"

"How else would I know about it? I was disappointed when the fire you set didn't kill her. She deserves to die. Why didn't you cut her throat before you started the fire?"

Dr. Evans looked first at Abe, then down at his hands. "I guess I didn't think of it. I thought she'd die a painful death before anyone even knew there *was* a fire. I wanted her to experience the pain I've felt all these years."

"I'm here to tell you she'll be giving you another chance to settle things."

"Is that what this visit is about?"

"Not exactly. I knew she'd make a try for some diamonds I had, so I got friends overseas to send me a little something to paint them with. That way, if she even touched them, she'd be infected with something that would kill her."

"I'm following so far. How do I figure into that?"

"What do you know about anthrax?"

On Monday Dr. Evans stopped again at the Samuelson's. Sally happily showed off her skill with crutches before settling on a sofa.

"Phooey," she said. "I'm here and my glass of water is over there." She moved to the edge of the sofa and tried to get up. "This is the hard part," she said.

"Allow me." Dr. Evans picked up her water glass and carried it across the room.

"Please put it on the end table while I fiddle with these crutches. You've mentioned a strapped leg brace. Any chance we can switch to that?"

"Why don't you stop at the office sometime this week? We'll get a new set of x-rays to see how your fracture is coming along. Then we can decide."

"Perfect," Sally said as a crutch tumbled to the floor. She struggled to retrieve it. "Getting rid of these crutches can't happen fast enough."

"Be sure to call ahead to let me know you're on the way."

"Perfect," Sally repeated. "If it was easier to get up, I'd see you to the door."

"I can let myself out." He got to his feet. "How's your neighbor Mrs. Perkins doing these days? Have house repairs started?"

"We haven't seen her since the fire." Sally lowered her voice to a whisper. "It looks like she drinks too much and knocked over a lighted candle."

"Is that how the fire started?"

"That's the rumor," Sally assured him as he headed for the door. When he'd driven away, she called, "Heather, I need you."

Heather hurried down the stairs. "I'll be glad when your leg is back to normal. Do you need your water glass refilled?" She reached for Sally's glass.

"Stop. Don't touch it. Dr. Evans' prints are on it. I called the department and they're sending someone to pick it up. I just need you to answer the door when they show up. They're taking it to the State Forensics Lab."

After Heather finished computer work for her clients she headed to Aba Brothers Electrical. Because Leonardo's activities were questionable, she'd volunteered to track him down and get answers.

"Leonardo has done such a good job for our homeowner's association," she lied to Aba's manager, "that I'd like to hire him for some personal work. Could I talk to him, please?"

"He's home today. His wife has the flu and he's taking care of her for a couple of days." The manager added, "We expect him back by the end of the week."

"I'll be out of town then. Could I call him at home? If he doesn't want the job, then I need to find another electrician."

"We can't give out personal information," the manager said. "I can't even tell you what Leonardo Pratt's full name is."

Heather gave the manager a startled look then said, "I understand the need to keep personal information from the general public. What I'll do is go home and write a letter to him. I'll mail it to this address." She took a step toward the door, then turned and winked at the manager.

He smiled, nodded, and turned back to the jumble of wires and electrical parts on his work table.

###

At the Pratt residence Leonardo's wife answered Heather's knock. "You want Nardo? I sick, so he at Save-A-Lot, then that bank next door. Maybe also the pharmacy. You understand?"

Heather nodded, thanked the ill woman, and drove across town to the Uptown Mall. With luck Leonardo would be easy to spot.

She went to the grocery first and found him in line with his purchases being totaled. She moved to the end of his aisle and waited while he handed a credit card to the cashier.

Heather heard her say, "We can't be too careful, you know, Mr. White. I'll need your identification."

White? Wasn't he Pratt?

The transaction completed and Leonardo wheeled his groceries to a sedan where he unloaded his purchases.

Intrigued by the name difference, Heather stayed out of sight. She watched him wheel his cart back to the store entrance and begin walking toward the bank.

Heather entered the bank, ready to wait and observe.

"May we help you?" asked a teller.

Heather paused. "I think I should talk to the manager."

"Take a seat over there." The teller indicated a waiting area and pressed a button. After a moment, a tall man with a neat crew cut joined Heather.

She said, "A man who is employed under the name of Pratt just used a credit card at Save-A-Lot in the name of White. I think he's headed here next."

At that moment Leonardo entered the bank and stepped up to a window.

"Hello, Mr. Costello," the teller said. "Back again?"

"I need to make another withdrawal," Leonardo replied. "I just spent all the money I had at the Save-A-Lot." He turned an empty pocket inside out, laughing as he did so.

"That's the man I'm talking about," Heather whispered to the manager as Leonardo pushed a withdrawal slip across the counter.

The teller smiled and said, "It's a formality, Mr. Costello, but as usual I have to see your identification."

The manager stood quickly. Customers had been calling the bank for months, complaining of money disappearing from their accounts.

The hooded figure seen in surveillance photos as withdrawals were made at ATMs up and down the West Coast had been the object of a frantic search. The manager nodded at security, and approached Leonardo just as he retrieved his driver's license from the teller.

"Sir, would you come with me, please," the bank manager said. A guard stood on either side of Leonardo, the jingle of handcuffs playing softly at their sides.

Leonardo said, "Why should I come with you? What's this about?"

"Just come with me and we'll talk in private."

Leonardo reluctantly accompanied the manager and the security guards into an office.

WHO'S SORRY NOW?

A, A, B, D, E, E, L, N, O, O, R

Using each of the above letters only once, add one to each word below, forming a new word. The addition may be at the beginning, end, or within the word. Place the added letter on the line below the boxes. The added letters, reading from left to right, will form a 3-letter and an 8-letter name that answers the title question.

lone	rave	hat
alone		

A _____

cur	thy	bard	the	rod	thee	one	fur
curl							

L _____

CHAPTER 20

Tuesday morning Inez called Heather. "I think you're right. I need to see a doctor about my hands."

"Didn't you go to the doctor after we talked at Doc Adam's memorial service?" Heather was at her desk, updating websites.

"I thought the rash would get better, but it's worse. And the lymph nodes under my arms and in my neck are swollen. Will you come with me?"

"I'll drive," Heather said, saving documents and turning off her computer. "Where are you?"

The staff at Good Samaritan's emergency room had been alerted to watch for patients with symptoms that included raised itchy bumps with black craters. Therefore, when Inez showed up, Dr. Evans was contacted immediately.

"Well, Mrs. Perkins," he said with a broad smile. "We meet again. Follow me and we'll get you examined." He turned to Heather. "I'll bring her back as fast as I can."

"Heather's coming with me," Inez said.

"Is she? Well, then, come along, Heather."

In the examination room Inez's hands and lymph nodes were checked, blood was drawn, and almost happily Dr. Evans broke the disquieting news. "You have been infected with anthrax," he announced, trying to smother a little giggle. "It's the first case I've ever seen."

"Anthrax?" Heather echoed. "Can you tell that even before you see the lab results?"

"I expect the lab will only confirm my diagnosis," Dr. Evans assured her, still smiling.

"Where would I contract anthrax?" Inez asked. "*How* would I contract it?"

"From the look of these welts on your hands, I'd say you came in contact with the spores four or five days ago. It's a contact form of the infection versus inhalation or gastro enteric. That means you handled something containing the spores." He turned his back to the woman and coughed, trying to muffle a giggle. "Probably you had open sores or scratches on your hands which the bacteria entered. Why don't you tell me where you've been this past week? Perhaps we can pinpoint the location of the bacterium. *Bacillus anthracis* isn't found just anywhere."

"I've been in town all week. I couldn't possibly have been exposed to anthrax."

"I wonder where in the local area you might have made contact with it? It may be," the doctor smiled and winked at his patient, "that you've handled something you were told not to touch."

Inez stared at him. Abe Coffman had said he didn't allow anyone to touch the Duchess Diamonds. Could Abe be responsible for this infection?

"We know," continued Dr. Evans, "there hasn't been an anthrax outbreak in Lewisburg or anywhere in Oregon. I'm going to have to confine you to an isolation unit until we make sure we have this disease under control. I'll have to notify the Center for Disease Control, and if you've waited too long for treatment," he swallowed what sounded like a nervous laugh, "it could be fatal."

"If the disease could be fatal, why are you smiling?" Heather asked.

"You'd have to be a doctor to understand, Heather. Now then, Mrs. Perkins. Let's get you isolated while I locate the proper medication."

When Heather got home she hurried to her computer to research anthrax. What she found was that it could not be spread directly from one human to another unless open sores were involved. In addition, the body's natural defenses destroyed low levels of exposure. The contact form of the disease, referred to as a cutaneous infection, was rarely fatal.

If that was true, why isolate Inez? Or, for that matter, why hospitalize her at all if she wasn't capable of spreading the infection?

Heather studied the computer screen, scanning anthrax documents, looking for clues she'd missed. If Dr. Evans tried to kill Inez once, would isolating her make it possible for him to try again?

"Jazz," Heather said when the deputy answered his phone. She was printing documents regarding the disease. "Meet me in the emergency room at Good Sam. I'll explain there. It's an emergency. We might need help." She hung up, grabbed her documents, and ran to her car. Among the information she'd printed was the name of the FDA-licensed vaccine. She'd make sure Dr. Evans gave Inez proper medication.

"What gives, Heather?" Jazz asked as they entered the emergency room at Good Sam.

"What do you know about anthrax?" She was breathing heavily from her rushed trip.

"Not a lot," he responded, accepting papers she pushed at him.

"Less than an hour ago, Dr. Evans diagnosed Inez with anthrax."

"Just by looking at her?"

"It's probably true that she's been infected, but she's not contagious. So why put her in isolation?"

Jazz said, "If he's the man who tried to kill her in the fire . . . ."

"Exactly. We've got to find her."

When hospital staff insisted law enforcement needed a warrant to take Inez from their lawful restraint and custody, Jazz called for backup with proper credentials.

"I should have stayed until I saw which floor Inez was being sent to," Heather said. "Do you have a friend who might tell us what we need to know?"

Jazz said, "The medical examiner might help if he knows we're trying to prevent a murder. I'll give him a call."

###

"I don't think this is a good idea," Jazz said a few minutes later as he and Heather got off the elevator on the fifth floor. The medical examiner had been in the middle of an autopsy and couldn't be disturbed. They were falling back on Heather's plan B until Jazz's backup could join them.

"If you can think of a better plan, sing out," she whispered. She'd borrowed a couple of colored pens from pediatrics. Her hands were now covered with spots that resembled those Inez had. She was also wearing a white mask over the lower half of her face.

They stopped at the nurses' station.

Heather coughed a few times. "I was told," cough, cough, "to check in at isolation, but I forgot which floor." Heather clutched Jazz's arm as if fighting a dizzy spell.

He said, "We're supposed to report to the unit where another patient, Inez Perkins, is already being treated for anthrax. Is this the right floor?"

The nurse took two steps away from them. "I didn't know we had a case of anthrax in the hospital." A huge shiver traveled her body. "We only have newborns on this floor. Contagious people are on three—3B, but don't move. I'll get you an escort."

"We'll manage," Jazz said as he and Heather hurried back to the elevator. On the third floor Heather repeated her performance.

"I think Dr. Evans is still with our first anthrax patient," the nurse said, keeping her distance from the couple. "It's that room to your right."

With Jazz at her side, Heather opened the door.

Inez was in one corner of the room, trapped by the wheeled bed she was trying to keep between herself and Dr. Evans. Currently he was crawling over the bed, a hypodermic needle in his right hand.

"He's trying to kill me," Inez yelled when she saw Heather.

"It's the vaccine for anthrax," laughed Dr. Evans hysterically. His laugh sounded like he was having trouble bringing it under control. "This woman will start a major epidemic if she doesn't get this shot." He hadn't taken his eyes off of his target.

"Hold it, doctor. Police," announced Jazz. "Stop where you are, or you're a dead man."

Dr. Evans turned and for the first time saw Jazz "Where's your gun?" he asked, turning back to Inez.

The door behind Jazz opened and his backup hurried into the room. "What's the story, Jazz," the deputy asked.

"It looks like Dr. Evans wants to kill Mrs. Perkins. Handcuff him, but watch out for that hypodermic he's got."

The doctor paused, then slowly backed off the bed. The hypodermic he'd been holding fell to the floor and his foot came crashing down on it.

"Oops," he said with a wide smile.

"Put your hands behind you, Dr. Evans," Jazz said, moving toward the doctor. He turned to the other deputy. "Grab a swab from that set-up tray and dip it into the fluid from the smashed needle."

Heather was pulling the bed away from Inez. "Get over here, Inez. You're coming with me."

"You can't take a contagious person out of my care," Dr. Evans shouted.

"She's not contagious," Heather answered, waving the anthrax documents at him. "You know she isn't. Why are you lying? What's gotten into you?"

"She stole the engagement ring being designed for my bride. Because of her, my entire life changed. Instead of life with the woman I loved, I've had nothing. This woman deserves to die. I wish Abe had found something more potent than anthrax to paint his damn diamonds with."

Dr. Evans looked at the deputy with the swab. "No need to run tests on that, fella. It's concentrated epinephrine. I was going to watch Babe's heart rate speed up until her heart exploded from her chest. Too bad you stopped me. Epinephrine probably wouldn't have shown up in the autopsy."

Jazz was talking into his shoulder radio, notifying his department of the situation.

"Bring him in," the sheriff replied. "We just got word it's his fingerprints on that alcohol bottle at the Perkins fire."

"Hands behind you," Jazz said to the doctor, grabbing one of his hands and twisting it behind him.

"Nothing in them," Dr. Evans responded, wiggling his fingers to display an empty hand. "I need a tissue for my nose, though." He pulled a tissue from a pocket, and quickly brought it up to his face.

"Stop him," Heather shouted. She'd glimpsed the capsule he was about to take.

Jazz grabbed for the doctor's hand, but it was too late. Whatever he put in his mouth was being swallowed.

Heather rushed to the door and shouted, "Help. We need help."

"Too late, Heather," sang the doctor. "Too late for me and too late for Mary Ellen." He was singing the words. "Tell her . . . ." A surprised look crossed his face. A moment later he crumpled to the floor.

Nurses rushed into the room and were at the doctor's side, looking for vital signs.

"Let's get out of here," Inez whispered to Heather. "You were right about who was trying to kill me, but," she lowered her voice, "I was right, too. Abe Coffman wants me dead."

###

WHAT IS KIKI'S NEXT MOVE?

To answer this question, follow directions for a three-word clue.

— — —   — — —   — — — — —

Start with letter X:
Move one space north.
Move two spaces north and two spaces west.
Move two spaces east.
Move one space west.
Move three spaces west and three spaces south.
Move three spaces north.
Move two spaces east and two spaces south.
Move one space east.
Move two spaces north and two spaces west
Move one space west and one space south.
Move four spaces east.

R	V	U	F	N
E	L	V	R	R
C	L	C	O	R
O	Y	S	D	X

CHAPTER 21

"If my front door is fixed, I'm going home," Inez said as she rode from the hospital with Heather. Jazz had stayed behind, waiting for investigators to process the scene of the doctor's death.

Heather said, "It was good of the immunologist to order anthrax vaccine and to give you antibiotics. He didn't seem to think your delay getting treatment is a problem. Obviously he saw no harm in releasing you."

Inez nodded. "Since I have to stick around, I'd like my key and my envelope back."

"We'll stop at my house and get them," Heather said, adding, "I was caught off guard when Dr. Evans said Abe Coffman applied anthrax spores to the Duchess Diamonds. If that's true, you'll need to have them sterilized before you handle them again."

"I'm betting some online research will tell me what I can do to solve that problem."

"You know you'll have to give them back."

Inez nodded. "For years I'd been promising Doc Adams I'd bring them for him to see. I'm glad I kept my promise before it was too late."

###

After the trip from the hospital, Heather went to her room to begin packing for her trip. She'd barely started when there was a knock at her bedroom door and Aunt Myrtle walked in.

"I brought you some tea," Myrtle said, setting the cup she was carrying on Heather's night stand. "Why do you have a suitcase out? Are you going somewhere?"

Heather pointed to the cluster of listening devices on her valance. "This is how I prepare a computer game for sale. I have to pack all of this information to go with it. There's a mailing deadline."

"I'm sorry, Heather. I didn't mean to sound nosey." Myrtle's hands balled into fists and moved to her hips. Clearly she *did* intend to be nosey. She took Heather's hand and pulled her into the hall, slamming the bedroom door. "Now then, I want to know what's really going on."

"Let's take our tea downstairs; then we'll talk."

Well out of range of all listening devices, Heather began, "When Mom died, she left unanswered questions. Because she asked that we not discuss them with anyone, Sally, Rachel and I have kept them to ourselves."

"And the trip you're getting ready to take will answer her questions?"

"It should answer one or two of them. When you were here in July, you discovered her September appointment. It's a reservation number. I tracked it down, and I'm going there for one night. It'll be a way for me to honor Mom's memory."

Myrtle sighed. "Heather Samuelson, do you think you're talking to one of Rachel's ten-year-olds? Do you think for one minute, I believe what you just told me? I want the truth. If the trip is to honor Mattie's memory, why is it a secret? And where are you going?"

Heather stalled, taking small sips from her teacup. "The fact is, we think Mom had a lover she met from time to time. I'm hoping he'll show up."

"And that's why you have a camera in your hands every time I look at you? You're taking family pictures to show some unknown lover who . . ." Myrtle stopped.

A flush crept up Heather's neck and moved into her cheeks.

"It's Charlie," Myrtle whispered. "You think he's still alive."

Heather didn't answer.

"You're not going to confirm that are you?" Myrtle smiled. "And Jazz is going along?"

"Not if I can help it."

"But he thinks you'll be in danger."

"Keep out of this, Aunt Myrtle. We think someone in law enforcement is working for Bishop."

"Well, we know it's not Jazz, so tell him where you're going."

"I can't. I won't. Please stay out of this."

"Deputy Finchum speaking," Jazz said, answering his phone.

"It's Myrtle. I want to thank you for your invitation to have coffee with you before I head home. I'm available anytime today."

Jazz laughed. Didn't any of the Samuelson women speak directly? Did they all talk in circles? What was wrong with calling to invite *him* to have coffee? And why did their mention of coffee always sound like an emergency was somehow involved?

"Perfect," Jazz sighed. He looked across the office at Sergeant Miller. "I'll see you in five minutes, Aunt Myrt." He hung up the phone.

"What's the aunt want?" Ox asked.

"Who knows, but since you and I want her to be our eyes and ears, this is our chance to put that plan in motion. I have the feeling the trip Heather won't discuss is about to take place."

At the coffee shop Myrtle sipped her white chocolate mocha, and looked across the table at Jazz. She spoke in a low voice, "We both know Heather's about to take a trip. I looked at her calendar and there's a reservation number written on the fifteenth of this month. Mattie put it there." She handed Jazz a copy of the number.

"Heather's leaving three days from now?"

Myrtle nodded. "That's right. And she won't tell me where she's headed."

"Why are you telling me?"

"Because I know you think she might be in danger." Myrtle leaned forward and whispered, "She wouldn't confirm it, but I think she expects to meet up with her dad."

"I thought he was dead," Jazz whispered back.

Myrtle shook her head. "I don't think he is."

"If Charlie's alive and Bishop's assassin is hoping Heather will lead him to her dad, then she'll definitely end up in the line of fire."

Myrtle nodded. "All her talk of Mattie having a lover is just so much hogwash. My sister would never consider a lover. That wasn't her style. She was early Victorian." Myrtle smiled. "She even insisted Rachel and Jason get married before spending any intimate time together."

"Did Mattie have that kind of control over her daughters?"

"She had subtle ways of applying pressure." Myrtle drank the last of her mocha. "Heather is more headstrong than the others. She'll do whatever suits her, and since the two of you are headed out of town . . . ." She winked at the young deputy.

He blushed. "Okay, so I'm going with Heather to keep her safe, but so far we don't have any idea where it is we're headed."

"My bedroom is in her office. I'll be searching her desk the next time she leaves the house. I'm betting I'll find a notation of some kind."

"Now that we know the travel date, I'll check with the airlines."

"Perfect. Between us, we'll discover where the two of you are going, but I have to add one important caution, Jazz. You have to keep all of this to yourself. Heather thinks someone in law enforcement is working for the other side."

As soon as Heather finished sorting the pictures she planned to take on her trip, she left for the county jail to see Leonardo Pratt. She wanted to know how many times he'd been in the Perkins house.

At the jail she buzzed for admittance. "My name is Heather Samuelson and I'd like to talk to Leonardo Pratt."

"One moment, please," a voice responded.

Heather waited, knowing Leonardo had the right to refuse visitors.

The unidentified speaker returned to the phone. "He won't see you. Write a letter. He might agree to read it."

With Heather at the jail, Jazz was using his official status to ask questions at Portland International. Now that he knew the date she was traveling, learning her destination was easy. Heather was flying to Baltimore.

"This lady's some kind of a celebrity, isn't she?" The airline employee who located Heather's itinerary looked excited. "Will we have paparazzi taking pictures?"

"What makes you think she's a celebrity?"

"Because of the major interest in her. Normally it's celebrities being tracked."

"You think because I asked about her that shows *major* interest?" Jazz shook his head.

"No. It's because you're the second cop asking for that information." The airline employee snickered. "She's a celebrity traveling incognito, isn't she?"

"I'm not free to confirm or deny that," Jazz responded. "Who else was asking?"

"Some big guy. He wore the same uniform as you. Are you two part of her security?"

Jazz winked at the clerk and booked a seat on Heather's plane. Was he duplicating Ox's work? Or, if the other man wanting information wasn't Ox, could it be Joel Bishop's assassin?

"Did you read that story in this morning's paper?" asked the man tracking Heather's flight information.

"You mean the one about the prominent doctor having a heart attack?"

The large man nodded. "He committed suicide."

"I suppose Dr. Evans made another attempt on Babe's life and she turned the tables. I don't suppose you've heard any new information from your sources?"

"Nothing that wasn't in the paper."

"Well, it doesn't matter now. It's time we got those listening devices out of the Samuelson house."

"The sister with the cast is going to the doctor later today. She can't drive. Her sister will take her, and I expect the aunt will go along. When they leave, I'll let myself in and remove everything."

"They've relocated the devices, so listen for music and head in that direction."

###

"Let's recap," Heather said to her family later that morning as they waited for the coffee to finish perking. Jazz had joined them. "Where are we with what's been happening now that Dr. Evans is dead?"

Jazz said, "We know he tried to kill Inez in the fire. His fingerprints are on the alcohol bottle he emptied. From what we've found in his apartment, he also burgled her house at least once."

"Leonardo refused to talk to me about his burglaries," Heather said, "but it looks like he set up that street light to allow him an opportunity to break into houses in total darkness."

"What's going to happen to Kiki?" Myrtle asked. "She's not a bad person. She doesn't deserve jail."

"She's been stealing things that aren't hers, Aunt Myrtle. There's no way she'll get out of this without jail time."

"You two," Myrtle pointed at Sally and Jazz. "You represent city and county law enforcement agencies. Figure something out. I don't want her in jail."

Sally looked at Jazz. "Inez didn't limit her activities to just my city. What about your county?"

"Same for me, Sally. She did her *shopping* overseas and in almost all of the fifty states. More laws apply to what she did than just Oregon's."

"Do not disappoint me." Myrtle stood, shaking her finger at the two law enforcement representatives. "I want her back in my life. You two see that it happens." She whirled and headed for the stairs.

Sally called, "I have an appointment with my new doctor in an hour. Are you coming with us?"

"No," Myrtle yelled.

Heather laughed. "If Aunt Myrtle steals things, she might get her wish."

"You mean the one where she said *I want Kiki back in my life?*"

Heather nodded. "They could be cellmates."

WATCH OUT FOR THE BAD GUYS

	1	2	3	4	5	6	7	8
A	Y	M	T	S	D	'	O	I
B	R	C	P	B	M	G	K	E
C	G	W	T	E	N	N	H	A
D	R	E	R	D	O	L	U	R

C3, C7, D2, A1   C8, D1, B8, C5, A6, A3

C8, D6, D6   D4, C4, C8, A5

CHAPTER 22

Myrtle left the family meeting because she had plans. When she got Kiki on the phone she said, "I'm ready, Kiki. Lay it on me." It felt good to be conspiring with someone her own age.

"You understand how we're going to play this, don't you?" Kiki said. "Thanks to that reservation number you found, I located the motel where Heather will be staying on the fifteenth. She's going to be at a motel in Dover, Delaware. I expect to be in an adjoining room."

"You told me you were taking a weapon," Myrtle reminded her in a whisper. "How are you going to get that past airport security?"

"It won't be a problem. As a courier I often carry a weapon."

"Will you be on Heather's plane?"

"Perhaps. She won't recognize me though."

"Heather's plenty smart. Make sure those moles and your blistered hands aren't visible."

"Count on it." Inez paused, "You're sure you're comfortable with all the doctoring I need?"

"I know you're sick, dear. I'll take care of you. You won't have to wear wigs to hide what that medicine is doing to you. You've got my Hudson address?"

"Memorized. I should be knocking on your door in a few days."

"Oh, Kiki, I'm so glad we found each other again."

"Me too, dear. Now then, we still have things to do before we start our new lives, so hang up. I've got some phone calls to make."

"It was good of you to take over Dr. Evans' patients," Sally said to Dr. Prentiss as the film of her fractured leg was being examined.

Heather had driven Sally to her appointment, leaving Aunt Myrtle at home, a fact that made Heather uneasy. When Myrtle did unpredictable things, it usually meant something was brewing.

"Your x-rays show good progress, Sally," Dr. Prentiss said. "I think we can go ahead and get rid of that cast and the crutches. We'll have you in a strapped leg brace within the hour."

"I'll be able to get along by myself, won't I?"

The doctor reached out to pat her patient's arm. "You'll have to take it slow and easy for a while, but you'll be able to manage without help."

Heather glanced at her watch. "Sally, since we live so close, I'm going home to do some computer work. I'll be back for you in an hour."

Sally waved. "I'll be the one dancing by the clinic's front door."

Heather did a double take when she arrived home. A car she didn't recognize was in her carport. Did her aunt have a guest? Was that why she was acting secretive?

Heather approached the front door and found it unlocked. She entered quietly and was about to head up the stairs when she heard a man speaking.

"That's more like it," he said. His gruff voice came from the second floor.

"Since I don't know you, will you be signing a receipt for that equipment?" Myrtle sounded like she was ready to burst into tears.

"I told you to keep quiet."

"I-I need to go to my room. I need to lie down."

"Stay put. I won't tell you a second time. Now shut up."

Heather backed down the stairs and quietly placed a call to 9-1-1. Knowing the police would come as fast as possible, she waited a minute, then called up the stairs, "Hi, Aunt Myrt. We're home. Heather will fix tea, but I'm going to the mailbox at the corner. A group of neighbors want me to talk about police procedures in view of our recent burglaries."

Heather hoped the idea that two people had returned and one of them was removing herself from danger would change the dynamics of whatever was taking place upstairs. She opened, then slammed the front door and began climbing the stairs. "While Sally's getting the mail, I'm going to change clothes. I'll fix tea in a minute." She knew introducing herself into the unknown situation was risky, but she couldn't leave Myrtle to face danger alone.

"Oh," she gasped as she entered her bedroom and took in the scene. Myrtle sat on the bed looking scared to death, while a broad-chested man in a police uniform gathered listening devices. "I didn't know we had company." Heather approached the big man, her hand extended to shake his. "You look familiar. I must know you. I'm Myrtle's niece, Heather. And you are?"

Ox stammered. "They sent me after this equipment. I'll be finished in a minute."

"Oh, Heather." Myrtle cast a worried look first at the officer and then at her niece.

Heather winked at her aunt and moved closer to the big man. "I'm glad you're removing those," she said. Her right hand was still waiting to shake his hand. "I know lots of people in the . . . ."

At that moment he turned and the name above his right pocket became visible.

"Sergeant Miller. Of course. That's why you look familiar. You're Jazz's partner."

Clearly shaken, Sergeant Miller shook Heather's hand. "I'll be finished in a minute," he said, and turned back to the drapes. "You pinned these babies pretty snuggly."

"He tore your curtain," Myrtle complained, easing away from the bed and moving toward Heather.

"It was an accident," Sergeant Miller responded. "The Department will pay for it if you file a claim."

A sound from downstairs made everyone turn. A voice called out, "Police." Footsteps pounded up the stairs.

"In here, officer," called Heather.

Two uniformed officers, guns drawn, entered Heather's bedroom. "What's going on? Who called in the B&E?"

"I did," Heather said. "I thought it sounded like my aunt was being threatened, but it seems Sergeant Miller was just frustrated because he tore one of my drapes. He's removing some listening devices someone installed."

"Getting a little rough with things, aren't you, Sarge?" asked one of the officers.

"Move aside," Ox replied stepping toward the doorway. "I've got what I came for."

His exit was blocked by the officers. "Are you ladies satisfied or do you want us to detain the sergeant with a few questions?"

"It's okay if he leaves," Heather said. She moved toward Ox. "Did you get all five of the devices?"

"Only three. I understand the others are in your kitchen. You care to show me where?"

Heather accompanied the deputy to the kitchen for the remaining devices. Ox got them, glared at Myrtle, then left with the other officers.

"Oh, Heather," Myrtle gasped. She held one shoe in her hand. "I was so scared. I thought that man was going to strike me, maybe even kill me."

"Tell me what happened." They moved to a comfortable sofa and sat down. Heather put her arm around her aunt.

"I was resting on my bed when the doorbell rang. At first I couldn't find my glasses, then, after I found them, I stopped to put my shoes on. The next thing I knew, that man was up the stairs and we were face to face."

"He let himself into the house?"

"When he saw me he said the door was unlocked, but you girls are so careful to lock it, I knew that couldn't be true."

"Even if it was *unlocked*, he didn't have the right to enter without announcing his presence." Heather puzzled over the sergeant's actions. "After you came face to face, what happened?"

"I had my radio on that station your iPod is set for. He came into my room and began examining the drapes. When he didn't find anything he asked where we had the listening devices. Before I could tell him, he grabbed my arm and pulled me to my feet." Myrtle rubbed her arm. "He was rough with me. When I said those machines were in your bedroom, he marched me across the hall. I only had one shoe on." Myrtle looked at the empty shoe in her hand, dropped it to the floor and slipped her foot into it. "After I pointed to those listening things, he told me to sit down and shut up. I wanted him to sign a receipt for the equipment and the torn drape, but he said he wasn't going to. That's when you showed up."

"Have you left anything out?"

Myrtle frowned. "No, that's it."

"Did you tell him we'd put devices in the kitchen?"

"To tell you the truth, I'd forgotten they weren't all in your bedroom."

The Sergeant had known the location of the fourth and fifth listening devices. Had Jazz told him? Or, was Jazz's partner one of the secret listeners?

"You got caught? Jeez. You were supposed to wait until everyone was gone."

"I rang the doorbell. No one came so I opened it. Everything was quiet so I went upstairs because I could hear that station we've been listening to."

"And?"

"And there was that aunt, still getting her shoes on. I made her tell me where the equipment was, and if those girls hadn't come back when they did, I'd probably have knocked the old bird in the head."

"Why didn't you knock all three of them in the head?"

*"The cops came. The **city** cops. They'd been called before I even knew the girls were back."*

"This situation keeps getting worse."

"Well, we have the equipment and that's what we wanted."

"Wrong! Since you said you'd been sent to remove the devices, then it's the county that ends up with the equipment."

"I never thought about that."

"We both need a vacation. It's a good thing we'll be taking one on Friday."

"I guess things in Lewisburg aren't exactly finished," Heather said when mochas had been ordered. She and Myrtle had just picked up Sally. The three of them were seated at a table in the back of the coffee shop.

"Are you going to speak to Jazz about his friend? Isn't it Miller who's the other half of Jazz's task force checking out the Joel Bishop matter?" Sally asked.

"It is. Jazz may have an explanation for what happened, but if he does, then I want to hear it. I couldn't ask him questions over the phone since he's sharing his office with that big ape."

"Do you trust Jazz?" Sally asked. "Is there any way he could be one of Bishop's men?"

Heather said, "I've trusted him almost since the day we first met. I'd hate to find out I could be that wrong about someone."

Myrtle interrupted. "Jazz is one of the good guys, but he ought to be keeping a suspicious eye on that fellow he shares space with."

"I feel almost like my old self," Sally said. "I expect to be able to drive myself to the office because it's such a short distance."

Myrtle said, "Since you're able to get around again, this is the time for me to tell you girls that I'm headed home on Friday."

"Home? Friday?" Heather looked at her aunt.

"Friday," Myrtle repeated. "The same day you're flying out, Heather. Now that Sally doesn't need us, we can both take vacations."

"Sally can't drive you to the Portland airport. She has to keep her driving to a minimum."

"You'll be taking me, dear. When you go for your early morning flight to Baltimore."

"How did you . . . ?" Heather stopped and sighed. "What about your friend? Are you leaving Inez to face the courts alone?"

Myrtle smiled. "When they arrest Kiki, you girls can expect me back."

Heather glanced at Sally and saw the expression on her face. "Why do Sally and I get the feeling you don't expect that day to come?"

"I have no idea why you'd think that," Myrtle said. "Let's go home. I need to start packing." She headed for the door of the coffee shop.

"Do you get the feeling something's going on we're not aware of?" Heather asked her sister.

Sally nodded. "I think by the time the District Attorney gets enough facts together to arrest Kiki, she'll be hard to find."

Heather nodded. "I bet the first place he should look is in Aunt Myrtle's apartment."

CHAPTER 23

"Heather, we need to talk." Jazz and Heather were just finishing dinner at a local restaurant. "We're coming down to the wire. I know you're flying east soon. I want to know what your final destination is." Myrtle had shared that it was Dover and not Baltimore, but Jazz wanted Heather to tell him.

"I can't tell you. Stop asking. Instead, let me ask you some questions." She had both elbows on the table with her cupped hands supporting her chin.

"Okay, shoot," Jazz said with a smile.

"Question number one. Would you trust Sergeant Miller with your life?"

"Wow! You don't pull any punches, do you?" Jazz studied Heather's face. "I suppose the answer to that is *I do*. Why?"

"Second question, would you trust Sergeant Miller with *my* life?"

Jazz could see her watching him carefully. He thought back to his stop at Portland International and the report that he was the second man tracking Heather. He'd asked Ox if he had anything new to share and Ox said he hadn't. Did his partner lie or was it someone else following Heather?

"While you consider your answer, let me tell you what happened earlier today." She told him what took place between Ox and Myrtle.

Jazz shook his head. "That doesn't sound like the man I know. I suspect Myrtle stretched her story a little."

"I was there for part of it. The frightened woman sitting on my bed wasn't there because she wanted to be. Trust me on that. You also can't tell me it's customary for police to walk into someone's house without announcing their presence, even if the door is standing wide open."

Jazz looked across the table at Heather. "None of that sounds like the man I know. I guess I can't answer your last question. Ox should certainly have announced himself before entering your house." It had been Ox who suggested the two of them work together to find Joel Bishop's hit man. Could Ox be a mole? Was his search not for a killer, but for people Bishop wanted killed?

"I have one last question," Heather said. "Why was your partner removing the listening devices from our house? Was it the county who install them?"

Heather's questions sent Jazz back to checking computer records the next morning. He began by researching the former partnership of Coffman and Miller, Jewelers. Highly motivated now, the search didn't take long.

Richard C. Miller had been a young father in 1969 when he partnered with Isaac Coffman to form a jewelry company. After the robbery in 1971, both partners declared bankruptcy. Richard tried to return to the jewelry trade alone, and when he wasn't able to, he grew despondent and committed suicide.

Jazz scrambled through in-house records looking for Ox's birth date. He found it. Ox, or R.C. Miller, Junior, had been twelve at the time of his father's death.

Jazz turned his computer off, and stared out the window. Ox's father had been linked to Abe Coffman's father. Were Abe and Ox linked just as their fathers had been? If Abe really scattered anthrax spores on the Duchess Diamonds, had Ox been aware of that? Could it be that Ox was looking for Inez Perkins for the same reason Dr. Evans had searched for her—to get revenge? But if his target was Inez, why track Heather?

Jazz moved away from his desk and started pacing.

At that moment Ox walked into the office. "Is something bugging you?"

"I'm just trying to fit puzzle pieces together."

"Anything I can help with?"

"It's too early to say. When I get a few more pieces in place, we'll compare notes."

Jazz continued his inner searching. How was anything Inez did connected to Heather? If Ox checked on Heather's flight status at

Portland International, why lie about it? She wasn't involved in jewel thefts.

Jazz left his office and walked down the hall. He stopped at the door to Lieutenant Hedges' office. "I need a couple days of personal time."

"We're short of manpower, and your partner beat you to it. You can't both take time off."

"Ox asked for time off?"

"He's trying to fill out retirement papers. That isn't something that happens overnight. The paper work these government groups come up with is enough to choke a horse."

"I want a couple of days off so I can work on some cases I think we're close to solving. Maybe I shouldn't have called it personal time. What I mean is I'm advising you that I'll be out of touch for a couple of days, but when I return, I expect to have a couple of cases solved."

"Can you be more specific?"

"You've known me since my first day on the job, Lieutenant. Can you trust me?"

"Is it something you and Ox are both working on?"

"Not that I know of."

Lieutenant Hedges studied Jazz, then said, "Two days. But that's all."

"Agreed. I'm leaving tomorrow."

On that same Thursday a Baltimore flight left Portland International with every seat filled. Passengers included an ill nun in first class and behind her, a burn victim accompanied by his heavy-set doctor.

When the plane landed, the nun rented a car and left town headed east. The burn victim and his doctor went to a jewelry store where they picked up clothes and supplies airport security wouldn't have allowed. They had roughly twenty-four hours before they needed to return to the airport and begin tracking a petite redhead from Lewisburg, Oregon.

###

On Friday another Baltimore flight left Portland International with every seat filled. This time passengers included a redhead from Lewisburg in coach, and boarding late, a tall, first class passenger in traditional Moroccan-style dress with a black mustache and beard. Eyes, uncomfortable in colored contacts, gave the normally blue color an irritated, watery appearance. This passenger sat by the window, ready for a few hours' sleep and some relief for his eyes.

When the plane landed the redhead got a small suitcase from overhead, then pushed her way through those greeting incoming passengers. Among that group stood a heavy-set man in modest attire, a gray beard askew on his chin, and a wool cap low over his forehead. Beside him stood a short man wearing a leather vest over a T-shirt, his arms swathed in tattoos.

At the car rental agency, as Heather loaded her suitcase, the heavy-set man with the gray beard bumped against her. He mumbled an apology, but kept going. Heather got in her car and headed out of the city, unaware that when the muscular man bumped her, it distracted her from seeing his buddy on the other side of her car, clamping a homing device under her right front fender. With that addition, her car now contained *two* homing devices.

Unaware of her popularity, Heather headed for Delaware.

Late that evening at Dover's Travelers Best Motel, Heather presented the room confirmation numbers she'd copied from her mother's calendar and her driver's license.

The clerk looked at the reservation number; then at Heather's identification. "That room is reserved for Ella Prince."

"I understand your confusion," Heather said. "I called two weeks ago to explain that my mother, now deceased, had your confirmation number on her calendar. I told you at that time I wanted to take her place. You can copy my driver's license, but please leave the reservation in my mom's name."

"We're sorry about your mother's death, but we'll need your identification, too. Will you want her mail and any phone calls?"

Heather felt her heart skip a beat. "Yes, please."

The clerk nodded. She handed a sealed envelope to Heather, gave her a key card to a second floor room, and wished her a good day.

Heather felt like running. She wanted to open the envelope immediately, and could hardly contain herself. On the third try she unlocked the door to room 200. Once inside she slammed the door, threw the dead bolt, and dashed to a chair. She was trembling.

The envelope, date stamped for Wednesday, was addressed to Ella Prince in a neat, bold style. It had obviously been delivered in person. Inside, in calligraphy, was the message: *Wait up. May be late. Traffic heavy.* The note had not been signed.

Heather checked her phone for messages; then ordered room service. When it arrived she found it difficult to eat. Her trip had been grueling and she was exhausted. After a few bites she settled back in a chair and watched the ten o'clock news. While she listened, she sorted through dozens of photos she'd brought to share with her dad.

The note had been right. Friday night traffic was heavy. Accidents were reported in several locations, with drivers warned to seek other ways of reaching their destinations. Heather sighed. Her father might be late, but she'd wait up if she had to spend the entire night in a chair.

That was her last thought before Saturday's bright sunshine woke her.

###

TIME TO BE CAREFUL

B - 1 =   G + 2 =   J + 4 =   Z - 3 =
J + 2 =   M + 6 =   J + 5 =   A + 4 =
O - 3 =   P + 4 =   N - 2 =
                                    H + 4 =

_ _ _   _ _   _ _ _   _ _ _ _

CHAPTER 24

With sunshine streaming through the motel windows, Heather leaped to her feet and turned off the TV. There were no message lights glowing from her telephone and the only item pushed under her door was a charge slip for the room and a reminder about check-out at eleven.

Heather showered and changed clothes, then repacked her suitcase in case she needed to leave in a hurry. What could her dad have in mind? How had these trips gone when her mother made them?

Heather picked up the phone and called room service again. She was afraid to leave the room for fear she'd miss a phone call or that special knock on her door. She ate breakfast and pushed her dirty dishes into the hallway. That's when she realized something in her room had changed.

The night before she'd placed her suitcase on the carpet near the door connecting her room to one on the other side of the wall. A paper sack with the uneaten orange she'd brought with her had been beside her suitcase, but sitting in front of the connecting door. The sack was now beside the wall perpendicular to the door.

While she slept, someone had opened the connecting door, and that movement scooted the sack to its new location. Heather rushed to the hall and knocked on the door of the room next to hers. When no one answered, she returned to her room and knocked on the connecting door. Again, no answer. She tried the doorknob. Locked. Grabbing the phone she called the desk and asked to be connected to room 202.

"Do you have a complaint?" asked the desk clerk.

"No. I expected someone to show up last night. I thought they might have stopped at the wrong door."

"The party in 202 has checked out."

"Could you give me a name or at least tell me if that person was male or female."

"I shouldn't respond, but I guess it won't hurt now that he's checked out."

"Was he alone?" Heather felt her stomach tighten. Who had opened that door and looked in on her?

"Yes."

"Thank you," Heather responded, still puzzled. "I'll be out of here on time, but probably not before."

Could her father have been in the adjoining room? Would a stranger have tried the door, found it unlocked, then opened it? Heather brushed her teeth, packed her toothbrush, then sat down to watch television as she waited for her mother's guest or the eleven o'clock check-out, whichever came first.

When news of politics flashed on the television Heather allowed her mind to wander. Would the person who delivered the note to the motel desk have left town? Surely they were aware her reservation had been made for only one night. Why wait so late to be in touch?

Heather picked up the envelope again. If the person who left the note Wednesday sent a floral arrangement to Mattie's memorial service, then he knew she was dead. He must have known it would be one of her daughters using the room.

The newscaster switched from politics to weekend traffic problems, recapping news of accidents and deaths that had taken place the night before. Cars traveling too close caused chain reactions. In addition, two long-haul truckers had died in a bizarre accident involving six vehicles. Witnesses reported hearing gunshots just before the pile up. Heather shivered and reached for the photographs she'd been sorting the previous evening, surprised to find a sheet of hotel stationery resting beside the pictures.

You're being followed, said the note. *I think it's Abe.*

Heather gasped. The handwriting wasn't familiar. Had she been so deeply asleep that a stranger actually *entered* her room? But if the note writer knew Abe, then the visitor wasn't a stranger.

Heather shook her head, puzzling over the events. Whoever entered her room had to be someone who knew her.

Jazz! Could it be Jazz? She picked up the phone and called the desk again. "Was the man who stayed in room 202 tall? I just wondered if it could have been my boyfriend."

"How tall?"

"Over six feet."

"Oh no. The man in 202 couldn't have been much over five feet."

"Thanks again. Sorry to bother you."

It hadn't been Jazz.

At eleven o'clock Heather left her room and took the elevator to the first floor to check out. "Would it be okay if I wait in the lobby for a while? Somehow I haven't connected with the party I expected."

The clerk nodded and Heather sat down in one of the lounge chair groupings separated by a collection of plastic shrubs. Another set of chairs lined the other side of the shrubs.

"No luck yet?" The speaker behind Heather hadn't turned around, but she recognized the voice.

"Jazz," she whispered, not turning. "How did you find me?"

"That's not important. What's important is whether you made the connection you expected."

"A note was delivered in person on Wednesday, but no one showed up last night. I don't know what to do."

"You mean you don't know whether to sit in the lobby for a couple of days or rebook a room?"

"Something like that."

"I think you should book a room and then you and I can take a trip."

"Where would we go?"

"Check in so we can leave your suitcase. We'll talk after that."

Jazz followed Heather to the room she'd just vacated. "Nice room," he said when she opened the door. "You should have seen the cramped facilities I had last night."

"I suppose that means you weren't in room 202."

"I wasn't even on this floor."

Heather fished in her purse and withdrew a piece of motel stationery. "Then you didn't leave this in my room after I fell asleep?"

Jazz glanced at the note, then at Heather's troubled face. He wrapped his arms around her. "I didn't. If I had, I would have signed it. Was it slipped under your door?"

She explained what she thought had happened. "Someone in room 202 opened the connecting door and it pushed the sack with my orange against the wall. They walked across the room and put the note on the end table."

"Do you sleep that soundly?"

"I was tired. Do you think Abe Coffman followed me to the East Coast? Why would he do that?"

"I don't have that answer, but that note means you have to be more aware of those around you."

"I wonder who had the room next to mine." She looked up at the man whose arms supported her. "Would the desk clerk tell you based on your law enforcement connections?"

"Let's go see. Grab all those pictures in case we get lucky."

At the desk Jazz produced his identification and asked to see registration information. He explained he'd made the trip east, following a suspected serial murderer. The clerk showed him the driver's license that had been photocopied when the occupant of room 202 checked in.

"Do you recognize this fellow," Jazz asked, handing the picture to Heather as they moved away from the desk clerk. The name on the license was Edward Applebee.

Heather studied the face with its slim, dark mustache and a hair tuft under the lower lip. She leaned against Jazz. "If this picture was without the mustache and the soul patch, would you recognize *her*?" She giggled.

"Her?" Jazz took another look at the picture. "Are you thinking this is Inez?"

"She's been insisting Abe wants her dead. If she's here, perhaps Abe has been following her and not me!"

"I'd be surprised if someone with Inez's abilities made a mistake about who Abe is following. If she says it's you, then I'm betting that's who he's tailing."

"Okay, next question." Heather gave Jazz a worried smile. "How could Inez end up in the room next to mine, and how could Abe follow me? I didn't tell even you where I was going. Only my sisters knew." She paused. "After the plane landed in Baltimore, I made the drive to Dover—in the dark. No one could have followed me; so, how did you end up here?"

Jazz smiled. "At the moment the tracking device someone put under your right front fender is en route to God knows where. It's on a newer car so whoever is tracking it, is following someone with more money than you have." Jazz looked at Heather's troubled expression. "Look, Honey. Let's run that errand I mentioned. Then we'll hole up in your room and figure some things out."

They handed the driver's license picture back to the desk clerk, thanked her and got into a car Jazz had rented.

"Where are we heading?"

"I spent the morning calling hospitals to see if any traffic accidents involved men in the fifty- to sixty-year-old range. There were two that fit that description. Since they weren't carrying any identification, you and I are going to look them over."

"Didn't they have driver's licenses?"

"Apparently not."

"I never thought about the possibility of Dad having a traffic accident. Are the men we're going to see in bad shape?"

"They're dead, Heather. We're going to the county morgue."

When Jazz and Heather received permission to view the deceased long-haul truckers, Heather held onto Jazz. Her eyes shimmered with unshed tears.

"I'd like to go in with you, if you'll let me," he said.

She nodded. "Thanks. I'd appreciate that."

"I think they'll have us look at pictures first. We'll only view the deceased if the picture identification is questionable."

Heather nodded, her hands clenched. Sally was the one who visited morgues, not Heather.

The picture she was given didn't look anything like her father, even accounting for eight years of not being with him—even considering possible plastic surgery. It simply wasn't Charlie. She gripped Jazz's arm. "Where's the picture of the other man?"

"Take a seat. I want to talk to the medical examiner for a minute."

Heather took a seat and accepted the cup of black coffee being offered to her, while Jazz joined the medical examiner in his office. He produced his credentials.

"Out of your jurisdiction, aren't you, Deputy Finchum?"

"I'm tracking suspects who've left Oregon. One of them is a serial killer."

"Have a seat," the examiner directed him. "How can I help you?"

"What's the C.O.D. Cause of death of the body we've just viewed? What size gun was used?"

"How d-did you . . . ?" The examiner stuttered.

"I track suspects for a living. I know the difference between a death due to a traffic accident and some other cause."

"I see. Let me check something first." The medical examiner looked again at Jazz's identification, then picked up the phone and dialed a number. When his connection went through, he said, "Just a minute." He punched a button on the phone and looked at Jazz. "Go ahead and talk."

"Who am I talking to?" Jazz asked.

"Jazz?" asked the voice on the speaker phone. "Is that you, Jazz?"

"Lieutenant Hedges?" Jazz responded. He scooted forward in his chair, prepared for the worst.

"Where the hell are you?" the Lieutenant shouted. "This is a long distance call."

Jazz made throat cutting motions to the medical examiner and with a smile the doctor broke the connection. "We members of law enforcement have to play it cool. Now then, in answer to your questions, it was a twenty-two caliber."

"News releases say there were two truckers who died. I'm assuming the other one is still alive."

"He was hit, but not fatally."

"I think the young lady with me would like to see if he's her father. I suspect he is."

"The name isn't the same and he didn't mention family connections in this area."

"She came with me from Oregon. They were supposed to meet last night."

"I see."

"If you're satisfied I'm who I say I am, will you cut to the chase and tell me what hospital the wounded trucker is in?"

The examiner wrote a note on the back of his business card and handed it to Jazz. "I suggest you tell the young lady as little as possible."

"Thanks for the information," Jazz said, pocketing the card. He returned to Heather.

"Are we finished here?" she asked. Her coffee cup was empty.

"For the time being. However, I think we'll make one more stop before heading back to the motel."

"I don't want to be gone too long. I don't want to miss my connection with Dad."

"You can trust me," Jazz said, taking her arm and heading for his car.

SHOULD HEATHER TRUST JAZZ?

	1	2	3	4	5	6	7	8
A	W	M	T	S	D	V	O	I
B	R	C	P	B	M	G	K	E
C	G	S	T	E	N	N	F	A
D	R	E	R	F	O	L	H	?

A1, D7, C8, A3   A5, D5, B8, C2   D7, D2
D7, C8, A6, D2   A8, C5   A2, A8, C5, A5, D8

– – – –   – – – –   – –   – – – –   – –   – – – – –

CHAPTER 25

The nurse at Saint Catherine's Hospital looked at the card the medical examiner had given Jazz. "I see you want to visit Eldon Prince."

"Can he receive visitors?" Jazz asked, his arm tenderly supporting Heather.

"Actually, he's been quite depressed. Maybe visitors will cheer him up." The nurse picked up the phone and spoke to someone, then wrote a room number on the medical examiner's card. "You'll need this when you get to his room." She initialed the card.

On the fifth floor Jazz and Heather made their way down the hall to an officer seated beside a door. He examined the card Jazz produced, asked for identification, then unlocked the door beside him.

Jazz and Heather entered a two-bed room where each of the beds was surrounded by curtains. Heather gave Jazz a questioning look. He nodded and she stepped forward to draw back the curtain on the first bed. It was empty.

She made her way to the second bed and drew back the curtain. The bed was empty, but it was being guarded by a second officer.

"Let's see your I.D.," he said. "Lay it on the table and keep your hands where I can see them."

Jazz and Heather withdrew their drivers' licenses and put them on the table. The officer looked them over carefully, then whispered into a radio on his left shoulder. After a pause, he gestured them to a connecting door behind him.

Slowly Jazz and Heather moved toward the door, uncertain what was ahead. In the next room they saw a man propped up in bed, his forehead and left shoulder covered in bandages.

"Heather," he whispered, tears gathering in his eyes.

"Dad!" She rushed forward. "It's really you. I so hoped it would be." Tears streamed down her face. "Where can I hug you without causing pain?"

Charlie Samuelson opened his arms and his oldest daughter walked into them. "I've been giving the Marshals hell. I thought you'd return to Lewisburg and I wouldn't get to be with you. I dropped off a note Wednesday as Jeff and I headed out for one more load. Did you get it?"

"I did." Heather paused, "And I recognized the handwriting. We girls guessed you were in Witness Protection."

"Mattie and I counted on you figuring things out. Joel Bishop's hit man hasn't been located yet, so anyone testifying against Bishop is still in danger. If his appeal puts him back on the street, then I'm one of the few left to testify against him. Once the feds find the hit man, we can all go home again."

"Oh Dad, I'm so sorry you had an accident and that your friend died."

Charlie Samuelson turned to look at Jazz, a question in his eyes.

Jazz nodded and said, "I'm Deputy James Finchum from the Madison County Sheriff's Office. They call me Jazz. As you've guessed, Heather doesn't have all the facts."

Charlie nodded and reached out to shake Jazz's hand. He could see the surprised look on his daughter's face.

"We should tell you, Sir, that Heather received a note from someone who entered her room last night while she was asleep. It says she's being followed by Abe Coffman. Does that name mean anything to you?"

"Only so far as recognizing him as a jeweler in Lewisburg. That isn't a name that came up at the Bishop trial. Why would he follow Heather?" Charlie looked puzzled.

"I suspect someone is hoping she'll lead them to you."

"My turn, you two," Heather said. "What is it I don't know? What are you keeping from me?"

Charlie nodded at Jazz. "Tell her." He seemed drained of energy.

"There was a murder attempt on your father last night. He and his partner were both shot."

"My God!" Heather gripped the side of the bed. "I thought your bandages were because of a car accident."

"We only have a few minutes, Heather. When we leave, you're going to have to give an award winning performance." Charlie gave a confirming nod to what Jazz said.

"I suppose I'm going to be in tears because none of the people in the traffic accidents, or murder attempts turned out to be my father."

"Quick, isn't she," laughed Charlie. "Give me another hug, child. Tell your sisters how much this is costing me to be without them and Mattie all these years. It was the only way to keep you safe, especially after that attempt on your mother's life."

Heather embraced her father again. Her lips brushed his neck. "Mom always said someone tried to kill her, but we didn't believe her. We thought she'd just been clumsy."

"I know. We didn't want to worry you. We decided that if I turned up dead Bishop would have no reason to attack any more of my family."

"I brought pictures." Heather said, handing them to her father.

"We have to leave, Heather," Jazz put his arm around her. "If anyone is timing you, it wouldn't take you long to know none of the people involved in accidents was your dad."

Charlie said, "The Marshals are close to identifying the hit man. I'll give them Coffman's name. I want to return to my real life. I've been declared dead twice now. I'm tired of reading my death notices."

As Jazz and Heather stepped into the crowded elevator, Heather wiped her tears. "I was so hoping there'd be someone I recognized among the injured." She hoped whoever the performance was for, appreciated it.

"Don't give up," Jazz said. They left the hospital and walked to his car. He opened the door for Heather, then moved to the other side. She'd barely gotten seated when he pulled her into his arms. "Oh Honey," he murmured, brushing his lips against hers. After a moment he pulled away and stared into Heather's startled eyes. "I'm so sorry we haven't found answers." He pulled her to him again and with his lips against her ear whispered, "Possible bugs in the car."

She nodded. When he released her she said, "We might as well head back to Oregon. I guess my father really is dead."

Jazz put the car in gear. "We won't be able to get any flights out tonight. Do you want to consider the fact that you've reserved a room and have no one to share it?"

"I don't understand," Heather said, puzzled at the change of subjects.

"Your room has two beds" he said, "and I don't have a room. Or a bed. See what you can come up with to solve those problems."

Heather studied Jazz's face. Her damp eyes were beginning to twinkle. "Now there's an idea."

"And?" he asked.

"Don't rush me, Jazz. I'm considering the various possibilities."

"Damn, I was hoping that Samuelson brat would lead us to her father." Abe Coffman turned to his companion as they followed Jazz's car, listening to the conversation between the deputy and Heather. They had recognized Jazz at the airport and had seen him remove their tracking device from Heather's car. The big gold Cadillac with their device attached had gone out of town without being followed.

"Those reporters said both truckers died. You think that isn't true? You think we killed two guys, neither of them Charlie Samuelson?"

"If Samuelson died last night, Heather would be in tears because she'd just viewed his corpse. Our information must have been wrong." Abe swerved to avoid a driver changing lanes. "I think Heather still expects her father to show up."

"I hope she's right, because if he does, I look forward to wasting him. Samuelson is the bum who sent my dad into a bankruptcy that depressed him so much he committed suicide. I've spent almost my whole life wanting to even the score." The hired killer's accomplice believed the false story he'd been told about Charlie.

It pleased Abe that his lies were accepted without question. There certainly was no point admitting the truth. He said, "Because we know Samuelson was one of the three men who robbed the trade fair, we need to keep focused on him. I'm not sure he's dead. As least not yet. Obviously we're going to have to test that possibility."

"How're we going to do that?"

"You can kill the kid. If her dad is still alive, that should bring him out of hiding. It did when I pushed the old lady down those cement stairs."

"I wish my father was still alive. I wish we could get his jewels back from Samuelson and turn back the clock."

"Your dad would be proud of you for wasting Samuelson."

"You think so?"

"I'm sure of it. When we get back to Lewisburg, you can polish off the Boston Babe, too."

Back at Travelers Best, Heather and Jazz entered room 200. Jazz put his finger to his lips and moved to the desk where he began writing: *The bad guys are desperate. No talking in this room. They may have put a listening device in.*

Heather nodded. "I wish we'd stopped for a late lunch."

"Grab your coat. We'll find a place on the other side of town." Jazz's dark blue eyes were laughing as they walked down the stairs and out the motel door. Across the divided highway from Travelers Best was a lunchroom. To make sure their conversation was private, they walked across the highway. Hopefully anyone with a listening device was waiting for their car to begin moving.

"Where do you want to start?" Jazz asked once they'd taken seats at a distance from other diners.

"My head is spinning. First tell me about your trip east."

"I was on your plane, keeping an eye on you."

"I didn't see you. Did you notice Inez or Abe on the plane?"

"No. It may be they took an earlier flight and waited for your arrival in Baltimore. Did anything unusual happen once you landed?"

"Not that I remember. I got my suitcase from overhead, picked up my car key, and drove straight here."

"Unless the paperwork for your car got into other hands, I'd guess something happened between getting a car key and driving from the lot."

"You mean like that man who bumped into me? He couldn't have planted anything. When he bumped me, he wasn't even close to my car." Heather nodded at the waitress as she served coffee.

"The tracking device was under your right front fender. Did the clumsy man have a buddy with him?" Jazz drank half of his coffee, glad for something to warm him.

"I didn't notice. I don't remember anyone."

"That's how I found you. As soon as the car was assigned to you, my contact inserted a tracking device and I just stayed behind until you arrived here. Thanks to Aunt Myrtle, I knew you were going to Dover and I traced your reservation number. I'm betting the same is true for Inez."

"I'm going to send that aunt of mine to a motel the next time she comes for a visit. She's definitely not trustworthy left alone in my office."

"Next subject." Jazz looked at his empty coffee cup and at Heather's full one. "Are you going to drink any of that?"

She pushed her coffee toward him. "Let's talk about the note left in my room. If Inez wrote it, then why is she here?"

"She might be following Abe."

"That makes it sound like a parade. I walk down the street with Abe following me and Inez following him."

"Something like that. Next question?"

"Abe Coffman? Why go out of his way to drive past my place in Lewisburg often enough to know when a different vehicle was parked there?"

"We know there's a connection between him and Inez. He has jewels and she steals them. What we don't know for sure is if there's a connection between Abe and Sergeant Miller."

"Your partner? I don't understand." The waitress delivered their salads and for a minute all talking stopped.

Finally Jazz filled Heather in on the Coffman-Miller history, beginning with their fathers.

Heather nodded her understanding. "Then Ox and Abe are related through deceased fathers who went bankrupt due to the 1971 robbery. But Inez didn't pull that. That was the robbery where her family got killed."

"That theft accounts for the relationship between Inez and Abe, and possibly Ox. It also gives me an idea." Jazz pulled out his cell phone and dialed a number.

"Lieutenant Hedges," came the reply.

"Do you know where Ox is?"

"Jazz Finchum! Don't you dare hang up on me this time! I want to know where the hell you are and when you're due back."

"You trust me and I trust you. I do not have time to explain. I need to know where Ox is. I think you'll find that information at Portland

International. Check on Abe Coffman while you're at it. I'll call back in fifteen minutes." Jazz's disconnect interrupted a garbled bit of explosive language at the other end of the line.

"Okay," Heather began. "We have Abe, Ox and Inez, all connected by jewel robberies—either as the robbed or the robber. Inez and I are connected because of her relationship with Aunt Myrtle and the accident involving Sally."

"So there's no reason for Abe to be interested in you. What's your history with him? Go back as far as you can remember."

"The first time I became aware of him was at Mom's memorial service. He came up to me while I was still in the receiving line and began telling me about the website he wanted me to design for him."

"That was last February?"

"Exactly. After Sally and I bought the townhouse he started calling fairly often, always after me to hurry with the website."

"You don't think he's just an eager businessman who wants to play online with the big boys?"

"Possibly."

"Did you ever complete the website for him?"

"I finished it last week. By the way, your fifteen minutes are up. Call Lieutenant Hedges back."

Jazz smiled and redialed. The response was: "Hedges! And this better be Finchum I'm talking to."

"It is. Where's Ox?"

"He and Abe Coffman left together on an early morning flight Thursday headed to Baltimore. That idiot traveled first class. Wait 'til I get my hands around his throat. He's probably charging the flight to the department."

"Check something else for me. See if you can get a look at Coffman's bank records."

"Why do I care?"

"Check for any large amounts of money that begin showing up after the Bishop trial."

The line was quiet. "Are you thinking Abe is working for Bishop?"

"Does it make sense to you that Bishop would hire someone already living in Lewisburg? Someone with a good reputation who could blend in? Someone who might need money after a robbery had him declaring bankruptcy?"

"You may be on to something, Finchum. Abe fits into the background like an old shoe."

Jazz laughed, "I think you've got your metaphors tangled, but all else fits."

"This will take longer. I can't get that kind of information in fifteen minutes."

"See what you can learn by dinnertime tonight—my dinnertime, not yours." Jazz broke the connection and signaled for the waitress to refresh his coffee.

Heather stared at him. "Do you really think it's been Abe all these years, murdering people? If that's true, he's the man who nearly killed my mother when she was pushed down a flight of stairs."

"I think that all the puzzle pieces are fitting together nicely. The reason Coffman is following you is because he's hoping you'll lead him to your dad. For some reason he's not sure Charlie is dead and it makes a difference to him."

"Do you think he was the guy who installed listening devices in my house."

"Possibly."

Heather thought back to who had removed those devices. "Is Ox helping Abe kill people? He's your partner. Where are his loyalties?"

"If push comes to shove, we may need to find out."

"If Abe is Bishop's assassin and he's still looking for my dad, is he apt to wait around, then follow me back to Lewisburg?"

"I don't think so." Jazz looked at Heather, wondering how much he could tell her. "I suspect Bishop's assassin, might make some kind of attempt on your life to draw your dad out of his hidey hole. That's why I'm hanging around. I'm your bodyguard."

Heather sighed. "I guess I have to remember that somewhere in the Dover bushes, lurks Abe, Ox and possibly Inez Perkins."

"Not just in the bushes. I think a couple of those characters came from under some particularly dirty rocks."

###

AND SO?

R + 5 =	M + 2 =	A + 5 =	D - 3 =	K + 2 =
D - 3 =	X - 3 =	Q - 2 =	R + 3 =	W + 2 =
N + 6 =	O + 5 =	Q + 1 =	K + 3 =	P + 2 =
A + 2 =			P + 4 =	Y - 5 =
D + 4 =				K + 1 =
				E + 0 =

<u>W</u> _ _ _   _ _ _   _ _ _   _ _ _ _   _ _ _ _ _ _

CHAPTER 26

In Heather's motel room, she and Jazz played gin rummy, waiting for dinnertime and the call back to Lieutenant Hedges. Time passed slowly and their tension increased as they waited for something to happen.

"I don't think anyone is going to show up, Heather. I think your mom just took trips because she liked to travel. I don't think she met anyone and certainly not your dad." He winked at Heather, reminding her that listening devices may have been installed during their absence.

"It makes me feel like I didn't know my mother as well as I thought I did."

"Change of focus," Jazz announced. He threw down his cards and pulled off his jacket. "I can't take any more gin rummy. I say we switch to poker. *Strip* poker!" He grinned wolfishly.

"Wait until I put a few more clothes on," Heather laughed. She looked across the table. "I suspect you're about to stop letting me win."

"You've got it, Hon. Wait till I chat with a friend of mine." He pulled out his cell phone and redialed Lieutenant Hedges.

"Just got the information you wanted, Finchum. You guessed right. Big deposits were made to Coffman's account after Bishop's trial. And they didn't come from Abe's insurance company. If he's back there with you, then you better keep your eyes open. For some reason Ox is traveling with him. Where are you?"

"Travelers Best in Dover."

"Delaware?"

"Thanks, Rube." Jazz hung up and nodded at Heather. He hoped the Lieutenant would recognize the call for help used by circus performers. "We nailed it," he said repositioning the small table on which they'd played cards. He wanted his back to a wall. Heather's too, if he could manage it.

"Let's order dinner in," Heather said.

Jazz had become serious after his phone call. He moved about the room, rearranging furniture. "Perfect," he said, still moving small pieces. "You order. I'm going to shave."

"Shave? Again? I don't understand." Heather laughed at the possibilities that crossed her mind.

"You will," he replied, winking at her. He turned on his electric razor and added it to a breast pocket in his shirt. He motioned to Heather to go ahead and order dinner as he pushed furniture to new locations.

Heather placed their order and hung up the phone. Her stomach was churning. She knew Jazz expected something serious to take place.

He moved to the bathroom door. "How long before they deliver," he shouted over the sound of the shaver.

"Fifteen minutes," Heather responded. *Was that when things were going to happen?* "Stop shaving and let's get this card game underway." She was wringing her hands. When she noticed Jazz watching her, she laughed nervously. "My hands are cold. I need to keep them busy."

He turned off his shaver and walked over to her. With his hands on her shoulders he looked into her eyes. "It's going to be all right," he whispered. "We'll make it through this. I'm not going to let anything bad happen to you."

"My impulse is to open that door and run screaming down the hallway. Instead," she pulled his head down to hers, still whispering, "I'm putting you in charge of my life." She kissed him.

"Just stay calm. Keep telling yourself we're rehearsing for a play. And if I tell you to drop, I want you flat on the floor immediately."

"I can do that. Now, let's stop whispering and get back to being *on stage.*" She smiled. "No fair," she shouted, getting back into her role. "You put more clothes on."

"Stop stalling and shuffle. It isn't just your hands that are going to get cold."

Heather picked up the deck and found nervous hands and fifty-two cards didn't go together. "Sorry," she laughed. "Those cards jumped right out of my hands."

"Never played strip poker before, have you?"

She winked at him. "That's not what I said." She giggled at his startled expression. She wanted their playful life to go on forever. Maybe when this was over . . . .

There was a knock at the door. "Room Service."

"Lights, camera, action," Jazz whispered, motioning Heather to the door. In his street voice he said, "You get dinner while I stack the deck." He was pleased to see Heather look through the peak hole before opening the door.

She turned to face him, a startled look on her face. "Ox," she mouthed.

Jazz nodded. He sat at the card table, his back to the wall, his Glock pointed at the door.

When Heather turned the doorknob, the door flew open, pushing her back into the room.

"Surprise," Ox said, pushing a cart with their dinner into the room. He kicked the door shut behind him.

"How're you doing, Ox?" Jazz asked. His voice showed no surprise.

Ox lifted lids from the food and stacked them together. Then he moved a pile of napkins and picked up the gun he'd tucked underneath. He pointed it at Heather. "Sorry, about this, Jazz," he said. "I gotta do something that brings that jewel stealing dad of hers out into the open. I'm gonna pay him back for my daddy's death."

"My dad isn't a jewel thief." Heather took a step back from Ox.

"You're wrong, lady. He and two of his buddies robbed Abe's dad and mine back in '71. It's time he paid for his crime."

"You're wrong, Ox," Jazz said. "Charlie Samuelson was an accountant, not a jewel thief. What he did was blow the whistle on Joel Bishop's crimes. That's why Abe wants Charlie dead, because he testified against Bishop. Samuelson didn't do jewel thefts."

"N-no. You're wrong. He got wealthy stealing stuff."

"Ox, have I ever lied to you?"

"N-no, but Abe hasn't either and Abe said . . . ."

The door behind Ox flew open, and Abe followed it into the room. "She's still standing, Ox. What's taking you so long?"

"Checking facts, Abe. Are we sure her dad . . . .

The bullet from Abe's gun caught Ox in the throat. The weapon he'd pointed at Heather dropped, and he followed it to the floor.

"Drop," yelled Jazz firing at Abe as the man leaped to his right. Jazz's bullet struck Abe's the left arm, but Abe returned fire, hitting Jazz in the right shoulder. The deputy's gun fell to the floor.

"Goodbye, Samuelson," Abe said, turning toward Heather. "Thanks for the dandy website." At that moment a body pushed through the connecting door between rooms. A young man, looking suspiciously like Inez Perkins, entered with a gun aimed at Abe's head. With a resounding crack it struck him. He dropped to the floor, and she kicked his gun away.

"Heather, help Jazz get his bleeding stopped. The 9-1-1 call I put in should have medics and cops here any minute."

Heather rushed to Jazz's side.

A siren sounded. "Gotta go, kiddies. There's a package for you at the front desk, Heather." Inez stepped through the connecting door and pulled it shut.

"Get Abe's gun," Jazz said. "Keep it trained on him while I check on Ox." Jazz's right shoulder bled profusely.

Heather grabbed Abe's gun, then rushed to the bathroom for a hand towel. "Take this," she said, giving Jazz the towel to use for a pressure bandage.

Jazz knelt beside Ox, checking for a pulse. There was none. He started to stand up, then changed his mind and sat down. "I guess I'm leaving all this in your hands, Heather," he said. "I don't feel so good."

"We're not identifying that stranger who saved us," Heather said.

Jazz nodded, but whether it was because he understood, or was fainting, she couldn't tell.

When the police arrived, Heather was seated beside the unconscious deputy, applying pressure to his shoulder. Also in the room lay one dead deputy and one injured jeweler nursing a concussion. Three guns were lined up beside Heather.

"Mom, Mom," shouted Tom Bennett. His twin brother danced beside him excitedly.

"They're talking about Aunt Heather on the television," Tim yelled. "I think she killed somebody."

Rachel rushed from the bedroom into the sitting room where Tim and Tom had been watching television. The news flash was just ending.

"Switch to one of the other networks," Rachel said. "They may be repeating the news."

Jason joined his wife and sons, throwing his arm protectively around Rachel's shoulder.

The commentator reporting the six-thirty news admitted to having very few facts other than a gun battle involving four Oregon residents had taken place in a Delaware motel room. A police officer was dead, another was wounded, and a Lewisburg jeweler suffered both a bullet wound and a concussion.

"It looks," said the commentator, "like the Wild West has temporarily moved East."

Rachel looked at her husband. He nodded. "I know, Honey." He held her close. "We're leaving for Dover, Delaware, in the morning. You and the boys pack. I'll make arrangements."

Rachel kissed her husband and started filling suitcases.

"My God!" Detective Sally Samuelson studied the television screen. Her lieutenant had just alerted her to a crisis involving her sister and three other Lewisburg residents.

Sally watched, trying to read between the lines. Somewhere in all that happened in Delaware was her father. Had Heather met with him? Was he safe?

"I've got to get to Delaware," Sally announced, directing dark thoughts at the strapped leg brace that slowed her down.

"Hold on, Samuelson," the lieutenant said. "There's a call for you from Madison County. A Lieutenant Hedges."

Sally grabbed the phone.

The man said, "I understand you're aware of the gun battle in Delaware involving two of our deputies, your sister, and Abe Coffman."

Sally could hardly sit still. "Get to the point," she thundered. "Is my sister all right?"

"She is. I was told you'd want to know that Jazz Finchum received a shoulder wound. The shooter was Abe Coffman. We suspect Abe . . . ."

"Save it. I already know. Is there anything more? Was any more of my family involved in what happened?"

"Not that we're aware of."

"Give me a number I can call."

Lieutenant Hedges sighed and gave Sally Jazz's cell phone number. "If you learn anything new, we'd like it if . . . ."

"Yeah, yeah. I'll let you know."

CHAPTER 27

"I'm calling to let you know your family is all right, but I can't stay on the phone. I need to disappear."

"Thanks, Kiki. I can never thank you enough for saving Heather and Jazz. Did anyone mention Charlie?" Myrtle paced the floor as she spoke.

"I wasn't there long enough to hear much. When I burst into that room everyone was either out cold, dead or in shock."

"When do you expect to get here?"

"Just as soon as I can drive the distance between Dover and Hudson."

Myrtle laughed. "Drive carefully. I've got your bed ready and waiting."

"Put a hot brick in it. There's a chill in the air."

###

Heather sat beside Jazz, now propped up in a hospital bed in Charlie Samuelson's fifth floor hospital room. She had given the U.S. Marshals the phone number for Lieutenant Hedges so their agencies could compare notes on investigations and searches for Joel Bishop's hit man. They seemed in agreement that Abe Coffman was who they'd been looking for, but until they were sure Charlie would have to stay in Witness Protection.

"I've sorted through these photographs about a million times," Charlie said quietly, looking at Heather. "Doing my job and being honest has cost me a great deal. I've missed seeing my grandsons growing up, and I've missed watching you girls get on with your lives. I'm tired of Witness Protection. I want to return to my real life."

Charlie looked at his eldest sitting beside Deputy Finchum. He could read the handwriting on the wall. He'd missed out on a big part of Rachel's life with Jason, but maybe he could be involved in Heather's new life with Jazz. He was still sorting details when the door connecting him to the real world opened once more. Two redheaded boys solemnly entered. "Tim! Tom!" Charlie whispered. "Give your grandpa a hug."

The boys climbed on Charlie's bed and threw their arms around him. "We've been missing you, Grandpa," one of them said.

"We promised Mom we'd never tell anyone we were here," explained his brother.

Charlie smiled and said, "I can't tell which one of you is Tim and which is Tom. Are you boys going to give me trouble the way your grandmother and her sister did?"

"You mean make you guess which of us is which?"

"That's what I mean."

"If we keep your secret, can you keep ours?"

"That sounds like a fair trade. What's your secret?"

"We'll tell you how to tell us apart." The boys leaned into Charlie's chest, one at each ear. They whispered their secret.

Charlie laughed. "No one else knows?"

"Nope!"

Still laughing, Charlie said, "Is your mom around?"

"I was hoping you'd remember me," Rachel teased from the doorway. "My turn, boys." She threw her arms around her father. "You remember Jason." She nodded toward her husband as he reached out to shake Charlie's hand.

"I see you've been taking good care of my girl and your boys," Charlie complimented him. "Thanks."

"My pleasure," Jason said, "and I mean that sincerely."

"I don't doubt it," Charlie laughed. "I wish Sally could be here, too. Is her leg healing?"

Heather said, "You'll be able to determine that for yourself. I understand she's on a jet and should be here after lunch."

Tears formed in Charlie's eyes. "I've missed you all so much. I've had to exist on pictures for eight years."

Heather pulled an envelope from her purse. "That reminds me, Rachel, this was left for you at the Travelers Best desk."

"Me? Who could have left it?" Rachel asked.

"Inez."

With a puzzled expression Rachel opened the envelope and removed a page. She gasped and handed it to Jason.

He read it quickly. "Can this be real?" he asked. "It says a Kevin Perkins Memorial Scholarship Foundation has been established at the state college in Lewisburg. It's to finance higher education for deserving students. The first recipients of this grant will be Tim and Tom Bennett."

"Good show," said Charlie.

Jazz started laughing.

"What's so funny?" Heather asked.

"Inez couldn't hand money to anyone. Authorities would know it was from the jewels she's stolen and recipients would have to give it back. Establishing a foundation means she can give the money away through them, and no one will connect it with jewel thefts."

###

Three days went by before Jazz was well enough to travel. After farewells to Charlie, he and Heather headed for Massachusetts, with Heather driving.

"Don't you think we should tell Myrtle we're coming?" Heather asked.

"Not if we want to see Inez again."

"You think she's hiding out at Myrtle's?"

Jazz nodded. "I think that's a good possibility."

"You're not going to arrest her, are you?"

"I'm out of my jurisdiction, but if she'll give me her word that she's through doing that hocus pocus shopping, then we'll forget about seeing her."

"Thanks, Jazz." Heather looked over at him lovingly.

"Keep your eyes on the road, Heather."

"No back seat driving." She laughed and tossed him a kiss.

"And keep both hands on the wheel." He grinned. "At least for now."

###

"Well, look who dropped in," Myrtle said. "Nice to see you two. You've been in the news a lot lately, but I'm glad things are quieting down." She motioned them to her sofa. "Tea? Would either of you like some tea?"

"Actually we've come to see that sick lady you've been nursing." Jazz watched Myrtle's reaction. She looked *hand-in-the-cookie-jar* guilty.

"I have no idea what you're talking about," Myrtle said, avoiding Jazz's eyes.

"Come on, auntie. Level with me," Jazz said.

"I'm not your auntie. I don't have to level with you."

"I've agreed to change that, Aunt Myrtle," Heather said, "so level with him." Heather smiled at her aunt and moved closer to Jazz.

"Thank goodness." Myrtle looked from Jazz to Heather and back at Jazz. "It took you long enough."

"I couldn't decide between Heather and you, Aunt Myrtle. That's what took so long."

"Well, I can understand that, and I forgive you for choosing Heather. You're probably too young for me anyway."

"Now then, auntie-of-mine, where is Inez?"

"I'm right here, Deputy Finchum," said a voice behind Jazz. "You look like you felt better than you did the last time I saw you."

"Why don't I get some tea for everyone?" Myrtle said, hurrying from the room.

"Heather and I owe our lives to Edward Applebee," Jazz said. "We can't thank him enough for what he did."

Heather nodded, a twinkle in her eyes.

Jazz continued, "All the Edward Applebee's in the world have been checked out and none of them looks like that driver's license picture the motel copied."

Inez nodded. "That's as it should be. Have you come here to do anything other than vacation, Deputy?"

"Not if you'll give me your word you're retiring from *shopping*."

"But I was so good at it." She smiled coyly at him.

"Listen, Inez. We know you have health problems. That may mean your skills will begin to slip. If they do, you know what will happen. I think the time has come for you to retire."

"And if I promise to retire, you'll forget where I'm living?"

"You have my word on it."

"Done." She smiled happily.

"Tea anyone?" Myrtle asked, entering the room with a tray that held only cookies. "If everyone is finished talking business, then help yourself while I show off some of the magic tricks Kiki has been teaching me."

Myrtle and Inez looked fondly at each other; then Inez turned and winked at Heather and Jazz.

"Myrtle's a quick study," Inez said. "And because she has *such good hands* . . ."

THE END

NOT ENOUGH PUZZLES?

More puzzles and mysteries can be found
in the fourth book of this series.
Follow the directions for discovering its title.

	1	2	3	4	5	6	7	8
A	M	F	T	E	E	W	L	D
B	D	U	H	B	A	T	B	C
C	K	C	S	S	J	X	Q	P
D	J	E	Z	Y	G	I	R	G
E	M	T	N	S	O	E	N	L
F	R	B	A	G	H	Y	I	N
G	O	C	T	Y	O	O	A	H
H	P	A	I	D	T	L	B	E

C2, B3, G7, E4, H3, E7, D5   C4, G8, F3, B1, G1, A6, E4

C _ _ _ _ _ _   _ _ _ _ _ _ _

PUZZLE SOLUTIONS

Page ix.   **HERE WE GO**

CHILLING MOTIVES PREVAIL

Page 5.   **ADVICE FOR THE SAMUELSONS**

STAY HOME AT NIGHT

Page 11.   **DANGER CREEPS CLOSER**

A KILLER IS CLOSE

Page 14.   **A LOOK AHEAD**

Missing word in the list is <u>MOLES</u>

A	C	C	I	C	H	A	R	C	I	N
W	A	E	D	B	E	I	L	R	E	D
D	R	N	S	I	A	L	L	E	M	U
E	N	T	H	O	P	R	R	E	D	R
H	I	T	M	P	N	I	E	R	V	E
T	R	N	A	E	C	T	H	I	E	S
A	I	L	E	E	A	P	S	E	C	R
L	M	O	S	S	C	E	S	S	T	E

Page 18.   **WHO NEEDS MONEY?**

Bone, three, read, beard = B R A D
Mice, road, year, brave, heat = M A Y B E

Page 21.   **WHAT TIME IS IT?**

TIME TO STOP THE MURDER

Page 26. GUESS WHO SHOWS UP NEXT

THAT HELPFUL AUNTIE

Page 33. A SEARCH GETS UNDERWAY

D<u>RA</u>GON	S<u>TAND</u>	M<u>ON</u>EY	PRO<u>BA</u>TION
S<u>HA</u>DES	N<u>EVE</u>R	J<u>AIL</u>S	OPE<u>RA</u>TION
<u>JEWE</u>LS	DE<u>PUTY</u>	K<u>ILL</u>S	PR<u>OTE</u>CTION

Page 42. WHAT'S GOING ON NOW?

Trace = T   Sport = P
Bride = R   Plan = L
Laid = I   Court = O
Cone = C   Tail = T
Knew = K
Every = E
Sport = R
Year = Y

Page 48. SOMEONE NEEDS SYMPATHY

POOR DR EVANS

Page 53. BEFORE AND AFTER

BUTTER <u>KNIFE</u> WOUND
BLACK <u>BEAR</u> CUB
DEAD <u>RIGHT</u> TURN
FLAG <u>SHIP</u> BOARD
FROG <u>PRINCE</u> CHARMING
FUNNY <u>MONEY</u> CLIP
HOUSE <u>FIRE</u> ENGINE
PUPPY <u>TAIL</u> END
MISPLACED <u>TRUST</u> DEED
RED <u>HERRING</u> BONE

SHOT <u>GUN</u> SHOT
WATCH <u>OUT</u> BOUND

Page 58. WHAT IS KIKI'S SIDELINE?

USING HER HANDS CLEVERLY

Page 64. THE TIME HAS COME

MAKE A LIST CHECK IT TWICE

Page 70. WORDS RELATING TO THE KEYES FAMILY

Cheat = C	Robe = E
Bead = A	Alone = A
Stalk = S	Seven = V
Three = H	Dead = E
	Seat = S
	Done = D
	Frog = R
	Court = O
	Plate = P

Page 78. WHO CARES?

ADDITIONAL	<u>MORE</u>	<u>M</u>
WAS ABLE	<u>COULD</u>	<u>U</u>
BLIND MICE	<u>THREE</u>	<u>R</u>
FIX EGGS	<u>DEVIL</u>	<u>D</u>
WASH AWAY	<u>ERODE</u>	<u>E</u>
PAL	<u>FRIEND</u>	<u>R</u>
ALL	<u>EVERY</u>	<u>E</u>
OVER COOK	<u>BURN</u>	<u>R</u>